Condor and Hummingbird

"A compelling and passionate novel about a woman's discovery that the most foreign country is within." Alice Walker

"Mysterious and clear all at the same time, and beautifully written." Grace Paley

"Written for 'the lost children of the world—not just of Colombia,' this first novel affectingly entwines the lives of three women (one an American, two Colombian) caught up in a struggle for freedom. Sisterhood—both practical and mystical—is the ideal that sustains them." *Ms.*

"Sincere, and written with a beautiful mastery of prose. What moved me most was its capturing of the Latin American world in all its poetry, but also its cruelties and contradictions. Luisa Valenzuela

". . . a gorgeously written and succinct novel which deals in intelligent and illuminating ways with issues of dislocation: cultural, linguistic, and familial. Her outsider status sharpens the perceptions of the protagonist, a young American wife and mother who has traveled into the turbulence of her husband's large family in Colombia. Via anxiety and loneliness, she comes to see her own culture and herself with greater clarity."
Janette Turner Hospital

"Charlotte [Zoe Walker's] style is lyrical, even mythical, and fragmentary. . . . [she] argues that a people's past is indelible, that each people has its own invincible and inescapable character, and that in each of us, regardless of our nationality, is a foreigner." *American Book Review*

"Laura finds in herself a new determination to overcome the obstacles of these dire circumstances, not by forging the violent revolution that she and her husband once fantasized, but a "small revolution." It would begin with . . . three women, three sisters, and it would be founded on love." Ana Castillo, *San Francisco Chronicle*

Walker's delicate prose, her gentle and compassionate vision, illuminate every page of this novel. Her heroine Laura's open-hearted embrace of life as she feels it should be lived, with grace and gratitude, does much to undo the harsh realities in which she finds herself in this foreign place with a man who no longer loves her, and his family which does not welcome her. Filled with wisdom and poetry, Walker's tale will become part of your own history." Merriill Joan Gerber

"Wonderful writing . . . captures the era perfectly." Daniel Menaker

CONDOR and HUMMINGBIRD

*For dear Alice,
What a joy to see your beautiful face—
dear friend and fellow writer! May your wings always soar!*

Charlotte Zoë Walker

*Love,
Charlotte
March 2016*

Leaf & Tendril Books
2016

First published by Alice Walker's Wild Tree Press,
Navarro, California, 1986.
Copyright 1986 Charlotte Méndez

Published in Great Britain by The Women's Press Limited 1987
A member of the Namara Group
34 Great Sutton Street, London

This third editon published by Leaf & Tendril Books, 2016
Copyright © 2016 Charlotte Zoë Walker
(formerly Charlotte Méndez)
ISBN-13 978-069250087-3

to the memory of
Josefina Méndez Mariño
lost sister

and for my children
David, Rebecca and Rachel

CONTENTS

"I do not know how to cure the fever;
all I know is to talk to god."

*Kogi priest of the Sierra Nevada
de Santa Marta, Colombia*

"All we know outside our daily life
comes from the dreams we have.
But we do not know what dreams are."

The Tasaday of Mindanao

CHAPTER 1

La Violencia and Love

It was the summer before the first Kennedy assassination, but we didn't know that. We had to go to Colombia to feel the gathering destruction, and the only hint of destruction from home that summer was the death of a President's baby, a small private death expanded into headlines. Later it seemed that everything was tainted with destruction—Viet Nam, the corrupted life of our country, and our personal lives as well. Only when I found a shared diary the other day, a worn notebook of love letters to my former husband (one or two from him to me), could I see that there had been love also. Not quite love, perhaps, but a straining towards it.

I do not know how to fit it in, that straining towards love. When I look back on Laura, I see a somewhat wooden girl, a dull one. A flash of spirit comes to her now and then, a reaching upward outward inward. But I do not see her searching into others' eyes—not at first, anyway. She is avoiding contact, and yet lamenting the absence of it. At first I thought she was well excused for this, for who around her was loving? Only Francisca, really—and Francisca was mad, or supposed to be. Andrés? No, you will see. Yet one cannot blame Andrés, though his reaching outward was always strained, veiled, uncertain—and easily withdrawn, as it often is with men. Sometimes I think the ancestors had devoured our power to love, eaten it to feed their disappointments. Would they ever bestow again, instead of devouring? And where did their disappointments begin?

In accident, perhaps. There is a story in the Alvarez family, dating back to the turn of the century. Claudio Rienza, a good Liberal, was standing with his sword in a doorway of one of Santa Marta's winding streets. The streets had been built like mazes to confuse invading pirates—but the windings had their uses even now. Claudio, young and gallant, was waiting for his enemy, the Conservative Juan Parra, to come along. When he recognized the step, he leaped out with a dextrous flick of the sword: an eye was gone before he ever saw the face. His own friend and fellow Liberal, Alejandro Alvarez.

"Oh, I am so sorry!" he cried out. "Oh, qué lástima, my friend! I thought you were Parra. I am so terribly sorry!" (Etiquette is an important part of the tale as it is handed down in the family.) Claudio pulled out his handkerchief to cover the wound and took his friend and fellow Liberal by the shoulders, guiding him to the doctor.

"It's all right, my friend," said Alejandro, as soon as he could speak. "I understand." They were Liberals and gentlemen, as the story always emphasized. The incident never marred their friendship—nor their inherited belief in political violence.

CHAPTER 2

Homecoming

It is the summer before the first Kennedy assassination. They have just come to Andrés's homeland, Laura for the first time. To them, America in the Kennedy years is a country of reviving hopes and Colombia the country of violence, the country Andrés left to find a new life, new dreams. They left Berkeley before People's Park and sheltered themselves from many omens in a small New York town where Andres taught economics in a private college. The Bay of Pigs disturbed them, but they made excuses. Everything was going to be all right. If we didn't have a baby, they would say to each other, we could join the Peace Corps.

True, when Kennedy announced the resumption of nuclear testing, Laura felt her hand tremble and begin writing messages of its own accord—automatic writing it was called. She'd read about it in a book once. On the night of Kennedy's speech Laura had just bought a case of dried milk to protect her baby and her little boy from strontium 90, and it was taking up space on the kitchen floor when the President's voice began to explain the new testing and Laura's hand to tremble as if filled with new electricity. Yet her hand did not write of violence when it wrote by itself, not then at least.

"God has given you a gift of love," it wrote. Laura did not believe in God. She looked around and did not see where the love could be—except between her and her children. Andrés said she should tell no one about what her hand wrote, for fear they think her mad. He suggested she go to Mass more often, though she wasn't a Catholic, and gave her a black lace shawl to wear in Church. She crumpled it up in the jumble of her dresser drawer, and he said she never appreciated anything he gave her. He dug it out for this trip to Bogotá, told her to iron it and bring it along. There would be many churches to go into.

At the airport they separated Andrés from Laura, which made her frightened and angry. She and the children pushed into a taxi, where they are wedged between his mother Pilar and the little pregnant sister Concha and her four-year-old son. Andrés striding off to another taxi with his two older sisters and Concha's German husband. Susan screaming, terrified, "Papá going, Papá going!," while five-year-old David calls out just "Papa! Papa!" But Andrés does not look back.

Laura tries to comfort them, her flushed, curly-haired toddler Susan on her lap, her serious, bespectacled little David standing on the floor of the car, clinging to her legs, his new glasses bumping against her knee, his lovely blond hair reduced to the manly crew cut his father had insisted on. Pilar reaches over suddenly and pulls Susan onto her lap. "Ay, nena, ay, niñita! Don't cry," she says roughly, bouncing her up and down. "Tucketa, tucketa, tucketa!" Laura pats Susan's shoulder with one hand, pulling gently at her with the other, hoping Pilar will let go, but then David is crawling into her lap, her little boy, and she hugs him tight. With her cheek against the top of Davy's sweet, shorn head, Laura looks reassuringly at her two-year-old in her strange grandmother's arms. She sees in Pilar's stoic cheek the same sad granite that she used to watch in Andrés's cheek as he stared straight ahead in the rushing Chicago subway, years before. Something caught at the heart—how can soft cheek be so stony, how can granite be so sad? Now and then a muscle would shift, a movement sad, remote and beautiful. She sees this now in Pilar as they rush past impossible green fields on the way to Bogotá. At the airport she kissed that hard cheek and found it soft as anguish. Susan continued to scream.

Concha laughs, saying something rapid that Laura can't understand. She is the youngest and prettiest daughter, Andrés's old playmate. All the sisters have elaborate poufed hairdos, but Concha's is dyed red as well. She has been married twice. The teenage boy who helped Andrés with the luggage was her son Pablo by the first marriage, and four-year-old Miguel is the son of Klaus, the fat, blond little man whom Laura instantly disliked. Concha laughs again and pushes her son to stand on the floor. "Say hello to your cousins," she tells him.

"Buenos Días," he says sweetly.

David grins. A boy almost his age! "Buenos Dias!" he says. Susan looks at Miguel with wet, startled eyes, and takes a long breath. "Good," says Pilar, abruptly handing her back to Laura, so that David slides to the floor and Miguel almost gets knocked over. Both boys giggle and steady themselves, wedged among the women's knees while the taxi careens along the roadway. Susan watches them in serious, expectant interest.

The women are all shy; Laura's years of college Spanish have gone blank for the moment. They look out the windows. The bright fields are gone already, and now they pass through a confusion of streets. All she can see with mental clarity are the burros—everywhere, little gray burros standing placidly, tied to carts full of one thing or another. "Look, David, look, Susie—donkeys. Burros." And people with dry, stoic faces, wearing rough ruanas. And hundreds of speeding, battered old cars.

After a long while they stop in a street of bars and small shops built into the bottom floors of colonial buildings. The white stucco, iron grills, tile roofs still rise above the commercial level with some of their old dignity. Laura, carrying Susan and holding David's hand, is led through a shabby doorway into a dim hall where paint is flaking from the walls. Up a winding stairway—is it one flight or three or four? This cold building, smelling of damp, cannot be Pilar's hotel where they are going to spend the summer! It is more like a prison. Maybe Pilar is getting rid of them, hiding them from Andrés. Will he ever find us? Will he look? It is a place of bad dreams, everything as cold inside as outside. No comfort anywhere. They open a door for her, saying something about rest, and leave her there.

Waiting for Andrés, Laura sits in the only chair, looking at the tall green shutters covering the windows along one wall, at the two mahogany wardrobe cases and at the three narrow beds, shoved into separate corners of the room by the heavy wardrobes. Susan dozes on one of the beds, while David explores the room, gazes out the window at the gray street below.

"You will die in Colombia, do not go." Her hand aches with a message, but she is afraid to let it write, afraid it will repeat the warnings that haunted her the week before they came. The message of the room is all the doom she can take in. They will be here all summer, in these separate beds, in this cold room. Already Andrés has been separated from them; he is not even here yet. And his mother will never like her, she can tell.

"Never mind," says Andrés when he comes in. "Pretend you are in the Peace Corps." He is very big on the Peace Corps. Also he can see nothing wrong. He is happy and excited to be home. After a short rest, to celebrate, he will take them out to see the place of Gaitán's assassination.

CHAPTER 3

The Wreath

In Colombia in 1963, "La Violencia" is still alive in the provinces, despite what politicians claim, and now that he has returned Andrés is remembering the political violence of his childhood. His own father threatened at gunpoint, another man's head exploded in front of their house when he was only six or seven, watching it all with unbelieving eyes. His father's quiet dignity, unperturbed by death as by anything. A man's head shattered in front of him—that was disturbing, but still he could turn the attackers away with forcefulness and dignity, soothe his family, and continue the rituals of his day as methodically as ever. Living always in history, he met the present as complacently as he read old chronicles. Andrés never forgot that; it became his own ideal.

Now his first ritual of homecoming is to take Laura to the memorial of an assassination. They stand in front of the large wreath that marks the place on this Bogotá sidewalk where Gaitán, the leftist hero, was shot in 1948. "This is where a great man died," he tells David earnestly, and Laura thinks, why do you have to tell him such things? Susan wriggles down from his arms to touch the flowers.

"No, baby," Andrés says, pulling her fingers away from the wreath and scooping her up again. He jiggles her up and down while he talks, to keep her from fussing.

"The moment he was shot," Andrés tells Laura, while David gazes up at him in wonderment, "the people seized the murderer and beat him to death. You wouldn't believe how *ready* they were for it. They took his naked body to the Presidential Palace and left it there."

"Andrés! Por favor!" Laura's glance follows the out-stretched fingers of Susan, leaning and stretching petulant-ly toward the wreath. She pats baby fingers absently, but she is thinking more of David, how can he take in such talk, how can she distract him from it? "Davy!" she says, "Look at this big wreath of flowers! How many flowers do you think it has?" And to her relief, he points his finger from flower to flower, counting. Maybe he will get to a hundred.

This rococo circle of flowers seems foreign to her, ex-cessive: in its own way, it understands the violence. But she is grateful to it for giving her little boy something else to think about. Andrés has told her many times before about the *Bogotazo,* the great uprising that came after Gaitán's murder. He has told her about Gaitán almost as if the man were a saint—though the pictures merely show a rather plump, somewhat young-looking man with a kind, preoc-cupied face.

"They say the murderer was a mystic, a Rosicrucian," Andrés says into her ear, letting her know that mystics are dangerous. She wants to ask him, is that what I am? A mys-tic? But she does not even believe in God. The "gift of love" touched her, the idea of it, but it wasn't real to her; it did not make any sense. She was more prepared for that other message, the one that came before they left home, saying "Do not go to Colombia, you will die in Colombia, do not go." But she has not mentioned that one to him. If she does not believe in God, why believe in doom? And she is mar-ried to Andrés; she had no choice but to come home with him.

They have always been strangers. Once an unexpected bond grew rapidly between them, resulting in a marriage. But they are strangers. She hopes in his country they will find something central, some core of meaning for their being together. So far, though, this first day, she has felt those words of warning her hand wrote more than she has felt her own heart's hope. Perhaps the warnings only came from her heart's fears. Or some kind of madness. She tries not to think. She doesn't think of the words all the time, but feels them in the desperate eyes she sees on the street, the desperate green of the fields and the mountains she saw from the taxi as they came from the airport. She feels them in this wreath for a dead hero, insistently fresh.

Laura turns to Andrés again, trying to call up her memory of his memory, what he would be thinking now. "*The Bogotazo*—that was when you defended the maid with that old family sword?"

"Yes. You remember. . . ." They stand uncertain on the sidewalk in the gray afternoon, their children at their feet. The memory is his, but she needs to be reminded of it, to sustain her effort of loving him. He was coming home from the University when it began. He raced along the streets aimlessly at first, a nimble boy just watching, half-invisible. The wild feeling, the screaming and running excited him. And he felt the rage over Gaitán, whom he idolized. He almost approved the fires and the sudden appearance of machetes, workers squatting at the curb to clean the blood off and hone their blades before rushing to the next expensive suit, the next banker or shopkeeper. It became like an ocean when you are pulled under by a big wave and hear its roar from within. When he felt the waves getting too big and the current becoming a riptide, he raced home. Marcia, the young maid, stood in the foyer as he let himself in.

"The cook and I are here alone," she whispered. "Your family is at the Gomez house and cannot return. You are to call and tell them you are safe."

After telephoning, he took the old sword down from the wall. The one old Claudio Rienza had used to put out the eye of Andrés's great grandfather. A consolation gift from Claudio, it had come with them from Santa Marta.

Now Andrés held it, balanced it lightly as he listened to the radio and to the sounds in the street. His own beloved hero dead—the new Liberator. Perhaps a Revolution would come of it.

When the two men broke in with their machetes, Marcia was in the little patio with her basket of wet laundry, standing on a tub so that she could reach the clothesline. Andrés stood in the shadows with his sword, thinking of heroism and watching her—how prettily she bent and stretched, how clumsily she had to move the tub along the floor from one spot to the next beneath the line. He thought how brave she was, to hang up laundry in a time like this.

They must have come in through the other skylight, appearing so suddenly they could glimpse this quietness before destroying it. Before they could approach her, Andrés was between them, holding out the sword. "This is a Liberal house," he told them. "You should go away."

"What good is a rich Liberal?" said the heavier man, the one smelling most of *aguardiente*. "Liberals are worthless!"

"We are not rich," said Andrés. "And she is only a maid. What could you have against her?" He had always run away from fights. He had just failed his first pre-med course because blood made him sick—yet after all he had seen today, this was the first moment that he felt a queasiness. He could feel himself trembling, but he held the sword as firm as he could.

The machetes were unsteady too. Gaitán dead only three hours, and already they were drunk. They did not know what to do with sorrow; a man was dead who had been their only hope. Great horrors had to pile up, that was all they knew. Extremes of horror. Andrés could feel this too.

"We are friends of Gaitán here," he said. "But I will fight you if I have to." At least his voice was deep enough. Maybe not steady, but for years now it had been deep enough.

The second man laughed and tugged the heavy one's shirt. "Let's go."

"The door is down those stairs," said Andrés. "I will follow you out." All this time he did not look at Marcia, but he heard her following him down the stairs. When the door was barred again, he turned around and saw she held the little garden fork in her hand. She dropped it and ran to him.

"I should have told him—what good is a *fat* Liberal?" Andrés said. "Or a fat revolutionary, or—whatever he was." He gave up the joke. She laughed a little, and then it turned into crying. That was when they began to love each other. He still felt ashamed, even now, that his parents had sent him to America when she was pregnant. They had sent her away first, without his knowing—pretending that nothing special was involved. But he should have shouted at them, broken through the pretense. He should have found her and married her, instead of going to America and leaving his country's troubles behind. If he wasn't a rich Liberal, he acted like one. His whole family did.

But this last memory belongs only to Andrés. Laura does not know this shame attached to the story. He has told her the part about the streets and the sword several times, because she likes to hear it, likes to think of him as a hero. In the Chicago days, when they had dinners with the Colombians there, his best friend used to take her aside and say, "Someday that man will be President of Colombia!"

And she believed him. That was under the dictatorship, when all the expatriates were dreaming of revolution. Andrés would walk with her under the university gargoyles and tell her of revolution. She thought she could be part of it, like Evita Perón. And he made her feel responsible, saying he would die if she did not marry him. And she was lonely, like him. And her father called from a thousand miles away, saying, "What the hell do you think you are doing?" Which left her no choice.

And now she is here. Or someone is here, in her body, answering to a name that seems to be hers, though slightly unfamiliar. Whoever she is, she does not understand anything. Where is the gift of love? And the Revolution?

"After the *Bogotazo*," Andrés says, "There was no hope. It could have become a revolution, but everyone got drunk and there were no good leaders. Then the politicians fixed everything as neat as they could. But in the countryside there was murder everywhere. Politically, there was no one who cared. And murders in the countryside just helped the politicians to avoid the issues."

"But you care," says Laura, automatically goodwife, but meaning it too.

"But I married you, and now we have David and Susita, and I have a safe job in America," he says. "What am I doing here right now? Just feathering my own nest—getting materials to write about Colonial economics. Soon we'll go back safe and comfortable again. Rich liberals!"

"Not exactly rich," says Laura. "Don't forget what it's going to be like, staying in your mother's hotel because we don't have any money."

He nods warily, as she brings them down from idealism.

"You know, you never did tell me what it would be like," she goes on, for her fear has built up and she has to say something. "I'm—a little frightened of it." For it is terrible. Cold, ugly, shabby. With travelling salesman types in the lobby and toilets with no seats. (The guests, his sister said, would steal the seats and carry them away in suitcases. A toilet seat fits neatly into the average suitcase and can be sold in provincial towns along with legitimate items like sewing machines and face creams.)

"I didn't know," he says. "Before my father died, the hotel was pretty good. How could I know my mother has had such a hard time managing it, and that my sisters don't help her?"

CHAPTER 4

How Laura Was Laid Claim To (In Old Chicago)

"Muñeca de palo, muñeca de trapo, murieca de plata," he chanted in her ears the while he kissed her, and she was lifted outside herself, became someone else. A beautiful woman she became, whose lover sang chants in a foreign tongue; an adventurous girl who threw away sadness and self.

She hated the taste of his smoky mouth. He kissed her powerfully through staleness in the strange Chicago places not yet familiar to her, for she had just come there. The first woman in her family to have a college degree, she had made this dizzying leap beyond it to something called graduate school, and wasn't sure. Perhaps it was too bold a leap, though she believed she could be anything, or almost believed it.

In the long tunnel of the subway at two in the morning, his chant echoed as he pressed her against the curving tile walls, and chewing gum wrappers scraped under her feet. "Muñeca de palo, muñeca de trapo, muñeca de plata." Stick doll, rag doll, silver doll. The chant was her transformation, her sudden richness. Inside the subway car, she would watch his stern profile as the walls of the tunnel roared past them. Stern and vulnerable, strong and yet about to cry. He stared straight ahead through his rimless rose glasses, and did not glance at her. He is so sure. He knows where we are going.

On the day she gave in, the Fourth of July, there were green leaves nodding through the window. She looked up at them from the dingy mattress on the floor. His radio droned a little chant, over and over it seemed:

Snark Super One Hundred Gasoline
Thousands say it's best
Largest selling independent gasoline
In the Middle West

High feminine voices in harmony, over and over, round and round in her head, gasoline angels. The other chant was gone, the Spanish phrases of seduction were gone.

"You are my wife," he said. "You are—my wife—you are—my wife—" Thousands—say—it's best.

The leaves nodded and beckoned. She was a silver doll—a rag doll—a stick doll. She was his wife.

CHAPTER 5

Tic-Tac-Toe

When they return from Gaitán's wreath, Andrés takes Laura and the children to meet his paralyzed aunt, Tía Marta. She lives in an iron bed in the middle of a dim, cluttered room. All the family crowds in to watch the glimmer of joy come to her pale blue eyes, as she meets her nephew's family, her delight at the children. But it's a rushed before-dinner meeting, confused and also sorrowful. For Andrés has not seen her since she was paralyzed, the day of his father's funeral. He has not been home since those two tragedies occurred. "So you don't remember me this way, Andrés?" she asks him gently. "No, Tía," he says.

"Well, you keep on with your memories. Remember me with legs," she smiles. She gave up her legs for grief. After Andrés's father died, on the day of his funeral, she ran wildly into the street as the women of small villages might do. But in Bogotá, on a busy street, such abandon has no place. And very little was gained by distracting the family from one grief to another, taking them from the cemetery to her bedside. But it could not be undone.

"Come," says Elena, breaking the small silence that has fallen on them. "I must show you where we eat."

"Yes, go eat," Tía Marta says. "I will still be here later." Andrés smiles at her and kisses her. Urged by their father, David first and then Susan summon courage to kiss their great aunt's cheek.

Elena leads them back up the spiral stairs, across the tiled hall floor and into a little garden patio.

"What a pretty garden," Laura tells her. "Qué lindo." It is the only brightness in the hotel.

Elena nods. While Concha is small and flirtatious, she is tall and elegant, an art historian who directs a small library and is quite well known. At forty, her dignity as a professional woman is established. She can afford to be disdainful now, of women who settle for marriage.

Elena comments on the garden, "Mamá and Francisca like to work with flowers. Mamá does not have time very often, but Francisca takes care of it." It is clear that Elena herself would never have time for a patio garden whose plants are kept in old cracker tins and olive oil cans, as well as earthen pots. Yet fuchsias and miniature oranges dangle prettily. "But come," Elena says, "Aquí es el comedor."

The dining room contains nine small tables set in three rows—the spaces in a game of tic-tac-toe. At one table two shabby, unfriendly men are sitting. At another, a muscular little man sits alone. His deeply lined face seems full of amiability. Half the creases turn into a smile as he greets them.

"Buenas noches, Señor Vargas," says Elena.

"Do we eat with the hotel guests?" asks Andrés.

"Sí." Elena walks to the middle table against the wall and sits down. There are condiments on this table only: a tin of olive oil, a silver salt shaker, a box of Scottish biscuits. "This table is mine," she says. "You may have this one next to it. Concha's family is on the other side."

"Where do Francisca and Mamá eat?" Laura hears the hurt in Andrés's voice, but Elena doesn't seem to. She unfolds her napkin and places it carefully in her lap.

"Sometimes with me, sometimes not. Mamá does not often take the time to eat sitting down. And Francisca. . ."

"We used to eat together." Andrés stands between the two tables, waiting. Waiting for the tables to regroup themselves, levitate, transform themselves into one long table with crystal water goblets, his father at the head of it, placid and dignified. His father imagining yet another table, with Simon Bolívar opposite him, earnestly explaining his hopes for the new nation.

"Sit down, Laura," Elena says. "Sit down, my little nephew! We will ask Mamá for cushions for the children."

"Gracias." Laura sits in the chair farthest from Elena, helps David to a chair on one side of her, then puts Susan in the one against the wall. Tic-tac-toe.

"Sí, Andrés." Elena looks at him again. "We used to eat together. But that was before Papá died. Things are more difficult now. And there is no private dining room."

"But at least we could put the family tables together," says Andrés. "I see they are all different heights, but I can saw off some legs and make them even."

"No," says Elena. "Mamá would not like it."

Concha clatters across the room in high heels, Miguel behind her. She puts him in the high chair beside her table, though he is clearly too big for it. He suffers being strapped in, but grins at his cousins who have no special chairs. Sitting down, Concha calls across to Laura and Andrés. "How do you like your room?"

"It's all right," says Andrés.

"All the rooms here are ugly," she laughs. "And I know about your beds. Do not think you can push them together. Mamá will only push them apart again! She did the same to Klaus and me. But look at me!" She laughs again and pats her pregnant front. Laura strains to follow all this, for the separate beds have frightened her. Their marriage is supposed to get better here, not worse. She never had a chance to find out what other men might be like, but lovemaking with Andrés touches great depths of sadness in her. Why, when she is close to coming, does he stop making love at once, as if it would be a sin? As if he is afraid of her ecstasy? She still has some hope that if they try and try, loving will get better, ecstasy will be allowed, life will make some kind of sense.

"Ah, but now Mamá has us in separate rooms," Concha is saying. She enjoys her audience. She likes to be the reckless woman and she is proud of having had to go all the way to Venezuela to get her divorce. Not many Colombian women have had the guts for that, Laura knows. She is very charming, too.

"Why do you stay here, then?" Laura asks her.

"Klaus! He would never give up something that is free. I beg Mamá to throw us out, but he charms her so much that she lets us stay." The maid is serving soup in heavy, flat bowls. Concha turns to scold Miguel. "Oh, m'hijito, do not eat before I fasten your bib! Rosa! You should know not to give him the soup directly. Always give it to me first."

"Si, Señora." The sweet, round-faced girl serves Elena and moves on to give Andrés and Laura their soup. She holds up a bowl for reach of the children, hesitating. "No," says Andrés. "Give it to me first. The child is not ready to eat. Where is the cushion you promised, Elena?"

"You want a cushion?" A strong voice from the doorway—Francisca, the middle sister, the one Laura met that tragic time in the United States. "I get you one," she says in her simple, proud English. She is nearly six feet tall, and her features too strong to be beautiful by ordinary standards—but now her hair is poufed up black and shining around her face in honor of Andrés's return. She is smiling gaily as she turns back toward her room.

Not the same desperate woman Laura remembers, who came to New York as a maid, against everyone's advice. Exploited and seduced—or raped- and sent home for crazy by the maid service, without her family being notified. That last weekend when she visited them, they should have known. Laura had to take her to the drugstore to find the biggest douche available, and then Francisca spent all day in the bathroom with it, explaining that she was diseased and could not get clean enough. They should have known, and in another week it was too late. An airline calling from Jamaica, saying, "We have a Francisca Alvarez who has been removed from the flight to Bogotá because of mental disturbance. What shall we do with her?" And the crooked maid service got away with all she had—the jewels in her suitcase, the money, everything.

The new, changed Francisca returns to the dining room with a worn brocade sofa cushion. She boxes with it at Señor Vargas as she passes. "Buenas noches, Señor," she sings at him. He looks up, smiling with the deep creases of his face.

"Do not play with me, Señorita," he says jokingly. "Take warning!" Francisca laughs and throws the pillow at him. Jumping up he catches it, then hesitates a moment, balancing propriety and glee on the edges of the pillow. Francisca dances over and catches the cushion, buffeting his face with it, then dodges away between the tables.

"Catch me," she calls, running into the patio.

"Oho, Francisca," he says, running after her. His good natured shouts and Francisca's loud laughter sound above the scrambling of their feet and the crashing of plants in the patio, then fade into the interior.

"Qué grosería," says Elena. "There is no dignity in this house. But it is all right," she adds for Andrés and Laura. "Señor Vargas is an honorable man."

"Are you sure of that?" inquires Concha. "I'm not! But poor Francisca, she needs some fun."

"You have a strange idea of fun," says Elena. "Do not forget that Señor Vargas is married." She picks up her personal can of olive oil and delicately shakes some drops of it into her soup. "Would you like some?" She passes the can to Andrés.

Señor Vargas appears in the doorway, holding the cushion flat on his palms. He walks solemnly to Laura. "For the niña, Señora. Please forgive the delay." He inclines his head slightly, smiling a little around the eyes, and returns to his table. Tic-tac-toe. Andrés lifts up Susan, while Laura arranges the pillow under her. Davy's chin is level with the edge of the table, but he sits there calmly, as if it's okay with him.

"We still need one for David," she whispers to Andres. "And another one for Susan."

Andrés nods at her. "Ahora," he says. It means "now," but she knows it is supposed to mean something like "in a minute," and at least with Andrés it often means much longer than that

"Rosa!" They hear Francisca's hoarse shout coming from her room. "Rosa-a-a-a!" The young girl thrusts the last bowl of soup in front of Señor Vargas, not stopping to see how it slops onto the table. She runs into the patio toward Francisca's room.

"How elegantly we begin your visit," says Elena. "Now she is going to demand supper in her room because she is embarrassed for her flirtation and because Señor Vargas either pinched her or did not pinch her. Who knows which?"

"No importa," says Andrés. "We will have many meals together."

Pilar comes to the kitchen doorway, stands there watching. Laura looks at her stern face, the hard cheeks and hooked nose, the eyes that conceal her affection. "Where is that lazy muchacha?" Pilar asks. "Dinner is ready to be served."

"Francisca has called her away, Mamá."

"Hmmmp!" Pilar turns back into the kitchen. She returns in a moment with two plates, which she brings to Andrés and Laura.

"On your first night home, your old mother serves you," she tells him. "That is not so bad, eh?"

"It is good, Mamá." He smiles at her. "And what is this?"

Pilar sits down on the vacant chair at their table. "Ubre. Made for your welcome. Eat! Eat!" She turns around and shouts for the maid. "Rosa! Come back here and serve the tables!"

Laura looks down at the greasy plate with its clump of wet rice, grayish beans, and large piece of pink-colored meat. "What is ubre?" she asks Andrés.

"I hungry, Mommy," Susan shouts.

"Me too," protests David. However brave he might be, whatever that is on his plate—it surely isn't food!

"Ay, niños, finish your soup first," says Pilar.

"Sí," says Andrés, "The children must eat all their soup before they get their meat and rice."

"You never insist on that at home," says Laura softly. "I'll just give them a bit of mine." Tic-tac-toe. "What is ubre, anyway?"

He grins at her, that sudden little-boy grin that comes over his long, somber face sometimes. "Cow udder. And you'd better eat it all, or my mother will be angry."

David looks at them in horror. He heard that! It's as much for him as for herself, when Laura says with an answering grin, "You can't make me!"

CHAPTER 6

The Family Jewels

Rosa-a-a! I scream until she comes and brings me my soup. Jorge Vargas is a stupid little man. I hate him. In America the men were tall, like me, and blond. I would have married one of them, if I could have stayed. I went disguised as a maid, but proud, with all my jewels, the emerald bracelet and ring, the diamond pin and the pearls, which Tía Marta gave me when I was a young girl hoping for marriage. She knew I would never find a husband, but she pretended.

In America, though, there might have been someone for me. I went disguised as a maid, but proud, with my jewels. They promised us we would not be maids for long, and many of us were from good families. We would have equal opportunity for all, and find our sweethearts.

But the doctor whose wife I was supposed to stoop for, he touched me with his evil touch and I could not get clean again. Again and again, I used the douche but I did not get clean. I must examine you, he said. If you have a disease we will have to send you back to South America. Ah, he knew I had no disease! And the Señora screamed at me for every little thing, because she knew. But it was not my fault; I did not want the ugly doctor. And I could not stoop for the ugly wife. I wanted to marry one of the beautiful tall men, and live in America forever, equal opportunity and no sadness, no people without legs in the streets, no murders in the countryside, just happiness.

But they stole my suitcase because I could not get clean, and when I tried to tell, they took me off the plane and put me in that hospital until Elena came to fly home with me, superior and offended as she always is, whenever I let my soul out, whenever I flap my condor wings.

But now my brother is here, and the sweet Laura. They can take me back with them, and I can begin again. Laura can go to the Ambassador and get back the jewels for me. Soon I will show them Monserrate, and light a candle to the Cristo there. O my dear Monserrate, my dear Colombia, what can I do? I cannot stand your sadness. I am paralyzed like poor Tía Marta in her room. All I can do is make a little needlework like she does, just as if I had no legs, no wings to my soul.

CHAPTER 7

The Jewels of Señor Vargas

Señor Vargas is in the kitchen with his torch, melting gold and pouring it into molds, making the crucifixes he sells to jewelers in small shops. The children stand around, as close as they dare come to the alarming flame, fascinated by the liquid gold and the little molds.

"They say La Violencia is over," he tells Laura, deftly pouring. "But they are wrong. I cannot even go home to my town without fearing for my life. My son cannot come here to visit me. And do you know why?" Señor Vargas is a dramatic speaker, always pausing for ringing questions. Laura enjoys it. Also, she likes him because he is the only radical around. Except maybe Andrés now and then, when he lets his heart speak. After all, Laura married him because he talked so rapturously of revolution.

"And do you know why?" Señor Vargas repeats, fixing her with his eager black eyes. "The government has given the people no hope. No *hope!* All it cares about is the comforts of the rich. What we need is a revolution. Not murders in the countryside—a revolution!" He turns up the blaze on his torch, smiling as Laura flinches.

She listens to him, wanting to add some words about the children. His torch hisses and roars, but she makes herself stand there to see what he will answer. What about all the children? She shows him the Bogotá newspaper she has been reading—the ads, classified ads for lost children! In

America a lost child would be front-page news. At least she thinks so. Señor Vargas nods abruptly, then spits.

"Do you think anybody cares about children here? A stolen child is nothing. A run-over child is nothing, a bump in the road. A hungry child—less than nothing." His torch spits as he turns it off. In silence he pours the streaming gold into the tiny molds. He seems to hate all the Spanish conquest ever stood for, yet he stoops there pouring the gold of ancient Indians into molds for little Spanish crucifixes, instruments of torture, while three small children look on in safety.

CHAPTER 8

Nothing

An evening out for Andrés and Laura. Rosa is in their room, watching the children. They go into a theater. Movie about a man who murders his wife. A sweet, feckless, boyish man with a ready grin, who murders his wife. Laura does not, of course, feel Andrés would ever murder her—but she recognizes something in the actor's charm. She feels she can trust no one. (You will die in Colombia do not go.)

On the way out, they meet a tiny child with a begging bowl. She is so young she can barely walk; her face is innocent and bright, a little weary. She is dressed quaintly, like a little gypsy, tiny wrinkled brown ruana on her shoulders, gathered red skirt that reaches to her bare feet. Gold earrings. Her brown eyes are frightened, yet almost merry.

"Don't give her anything," says Andrés.

"But why?"

"Look—her parents are there leaning against the wall. Do you want to encourage them to use her like this?"

Both of them avoid Laura's glance. Then the man changes his mind, sends her an angry, shamed, defensive look from clear, dark eyes. The woman watches the child sadly. The little girl runs back to her parents. Can we go home now?

A father and mother, seemingly whole. But what is wholeness? How much wholeness is allowed? They turn the child around and send her back again. Other customers are emerging from the theater. It is not yet midnight.

CHAPTER 9

Elena's Jewels

Elena has her own jewel box—she is curator of a small museum and library of native Colombian art, maintained by one of the banks for the sake of prestige and public relations. *This* is Elena's home, Laura sees, when Francisca takes her and the children to visit the library. Andrés, as usual, is spending his day in the archives, gathering microfilm for his research.

Elena's influence is evident in the library's décor—the cool, deep blue draperies and carpets, teak cabinets, white walls, and elegantly contemporary chairs and sofas of deeper, midnight blue. The golden artifacts gleam in glass cases; the pottery absorbs light and time, surrounding itself with a hazy aura, and the books in the tall shelves glow with many-colored bindings. Elena has a Beethoven trio playing on the stereo.

"This is wonderful!" says Laura.

Elena nods with austere pride. "Let me show you a few things." Taking a key from the drawer of her desk, she opens the nearest glass case and removes a small golden decanter, perfectly harmonized in shape, with four golden balls forming the stopper. She puts it into Laura's hand. "Feel the balance of this," she says. "Perfection."

"Yes." Laura absorbs the lovely form and balance for a few moments, then hands the piece back reverently.

"Quimbaya," calls out Francisca. "From near Antioquia." She is holding David by the hand, leading him to the display of golden animals—frogs, lizards, birds. Laura sees her little boy's eyes brighten with amazement and delight, and walks to the display with Susan, so both can see it.

"How did you know?" she asks Francisca.

"Francisca has begun studying here recently," Elena answers for her. "I tell her she should study for a degree, like I did." She locks the decanter away.

"That would take all the joy out of it," says Francisca brusquely. "Anyway, I cannot imitate you, Elena. I only read when I want to, about my Indios."

As if avoiding argument, Elena walks further along the wall of Indian objects.

"Show Laura something of the Tairona," says Francisca. "Those are *my* people."

"Here is something," Elena responds. Laura picks up Susan again and follows her to look inside the case at a sort of Humpty Dumpty who never broke, an egg-shaped clay fellow with a removable top.

"What is it?" Laura asks.

"An effigy burial urn—from the Tairona. Francisca loves the Tairona because they are from near our home—from the Sierra Nevada de Santa Marta."

Francisca comes to stand beside them, holding David's hand. "Also because they refused to be enslaved," she says. "They went high in the mountains and no one could touch them."

"The Tairona *were* magnificent," says Elena. "Look." She pulls a book from one of the shelves and quickly turns to a section of diagrams. "You see—they left wonderful ruins. Simple, but very intelligent. Such staircases! Now their descendants, the Kogi, build round huts very much like these."

Laura looks at the pictures offered her, but she is thinking more of this surprising interest of Francisca's. Somehow, she has assumed Francisca had nothing like this, no special interest. It is Francisca whose eyes she meets as she looks up from the book. "I would like to learn more about them," she says. "About their beliefs and their myths, too."

Abruptly Francisca's face clouds over. "Elena will teach you," she says. "I do not know anything." She drops Susan's hand and walks swiftly to the opposite side of the room. She pauses a moment near the door, then turns around briefly. "I will wait for you outside." She slams the door.

"Never mind," says Elena. "Francisca is difficult sometimes."

Susan goes running across the room after her. "'Cisca! 'Cisca, wait!"

Elena rushes after, swooping her up in a swift movement that Laura likes—something more natural than Elena's usual measured gestures. "Come with Tía 'Lena, Susita. Come, David!"—she pronounces it Dah-veed, the way Andrés always does—"I want to show you something."

Laura feels anxious as she closes the book and puts it back on the shelf. What has she said to make Francisca so upset? She follows Elena and the children to a display case where Elena is explaining a clay sculpture to them. "You see, Susita, it is a ball game. See the players in the center, David? And look, here is a little child sitting on his Papá's lap. And here is another one with his Papá's arm around him. Just like the two of you!"

"Look, Mama," says David. "It's really, really old, and they used to play ball, and somebody made it out of clay!"

"Look, Mom," says Susan in her precocious way, peering up for Laura's approval.

"Yes," she smiles at both of them. "Isn't it great?" And it is. It's amazing, this ancient miniature sculpture of a game that could almost take place in the town ball park at home. Bleachers with little clay figures in various attitudes—jeering old men, parents and children, lovers with their arms around each other, watching athletes in the little playing field.

"If I had some clay, I bet I could make one too," says David."

"Maybe we can find some," she says, wondering if it's possible. Are there art stores in Bogotá? Toy stores?

Still, Laura's mind is with Francisca, and she wishes Elena would say more. "Maybe we should go now," she suggests.

"Go find 'Cisca," says Susan.

"Maybe so," Elena agrees. "You see, Francisca is very interested in the Indians—in a very personal way. But she resents me for finding them first. Even though my interest is very different from hers—more purely aesthetic, more professional. But—you can see how she feels! And Laura—when you asked her about the myths. They are what she knows best. But they are very personal to her, almost as if she believed them—or no, more as if she made them up herself. I wish she would see the difference—I am not interested in things in the same way she is. There is no competition."

"But you have this beautiful library," says Laura. "And you can open the display cases with your own key, and take out those priceless objects when you like—"

Elena frowns at her a little. "I have worked hard for it," is all she says.

Laura thinks about Francisca, making up the myths of her *Indios*.

CHAPTER 10

The Origin of Dreams

There was a man who left the forest of his own tribe to seek his fortune. He found himself wandering in a strange forest and could not remember who he was. It seemed to him an unfriendly place. Jaguars and other creatures would leap at him from the trees, so that sometimes he had to change into a tortoise in order to protect himself. This made it even harder for him to remember who he was.

He met an owl who was kind to him, and they were married. But the owl kept calling "Who? Who?" whenever he went to sleep. This made him nervous, but it also caused him to remember his own forest, so he took the owl woman back there with him. Still, she called "Who? Who?" and he had no answer. Other creatures came in his sleep—the macaw, the condor, the bird of paradise. They began asking other questions: "When? Where? Why?" He began to make answer-pictures in his sleep. And when he woke, he would remember the answer-pictures, and his mind would be more at ease. But he did not speak of them to anyone, for he realized that to tell them would be to give others power over himself.

So he kept the answer-pictures inside him, where they hummed quietly, and multiplied. When there were too many, he would open his mouth on a moonless night, and they would fly upward to become stars. Still, more answer-pictures took form and hummed inside him, and some of them longed to be words instead of stars, and so they crowded and hummed in his chest and throat and just behind his tongue. Someday he would find the friends he could trust, and then he would tell them the pictures that turned into stars, and at last into words.

CHAPTER 11

Monserrate

Andrés gazes down at the mountain unfurling beneath him. He stands at a steep angle in the back of the funicular, the same cog railway car he took up this mountain from Bogotá when he was a boy. In those days, excursions had been more pleasant—for he would be unnoticed and free to respond to things or not, as it pleased him. Now they are too involved, too many people have to be considered. But today Francisca has organized most of it. Laura and Susan, his two gringas, have been quiet, a little frightened by the steep ride, and David, as usual, is gazing at everything, trying to take it all in; now that he can see better with his new glasses, he looks even more serious, more observant—more like me, Andrés thinks. Pleased, comforted, he begins to settle into his own thoughts and memories for the first time since coming home to Bogotá. He feels strange, suspended between the two countries, like this funicular hanging on the mountainside, moving so dizzily.

I remember my first ride up the funicular as a boy of twelve. We had just moved to Bogotá from the coast, and I was very sick. It was so damp, so cold in the streets, in the house, even between the sheets of my hard bed. Andrés grips the pole, which is all that keeps him from tumbling out of the car and rolling down the mountainside. As a boy he used to cling to it with both hands, releasing one hand now and then to lean out with arm extended, trying to taste the feeling of fall. In another year or so, David would do the same. (Papá would bring a paper and read most of the ride, never noticing my tricks. He could always be depended on to lose himself in words and leave me free for a little mischief.)

"How green it all is!" Laura's American voice breaks into Spanish thoughts. Andrés nods. The slopes are as green as the emeralds from Colombian mines. Green inside the earth and green on top of it. He has not thought of it until now, how nothing in the United States is as green as these mountains, or the llanos outside the city.

"Pelo verde y venas verdes—Colombia!" says Francisca, rolling out the words. He is startled, having her come so close to his thoughts.

Laura looks at him inquiringly. Her Spanish ear is not yet tuned to metaphor. "She says Colombia has green skin and green veins," he tells her. "She means the grass on the mountains and the emeralds in the mines." Laura is the tourist, and he is the native guide. Now *she* is the foreigner, he realizes suddenly—almost the intruder.

"Is it from a poem?" she asks.

"It is only from Francisca," his sister answers shyly, in English.

A loud grinding noise startles them as they enter the final stage of the lift; they pass through a dark concrete structure, then stop with a harsh digging in of brakes and gears. It sounds the same as on Andrés's first boyhood ride—as if the whole thing were about to slip and go careening backward, hurling itself like a meteor into the center of Bogotá.

Susan and Laura cling together, mother and child with faces alike, trying to hide their fear. David grins with delight. Francisca laughs.

"You think we go down the hill again! You too, my brother! So funny!" She stands up. "Here, I carry Susan out," she adds, reaching for her.

Andrés watches Laura draw back protectively—why is she so mistrustful? As if his sister does not love Susita too!

"Here, I'll take her," he says, while Laura takes hold of her little boy's hand.

"We must go first to the Church of Monserrate," says Francisca, "and pray God the car will not fall on the way down!" She laughs again; this time they all laugh.

A group of *gamines,* street urchins from Bogotá, crowd about the passengers as they get off the funicular. These tough, homeless ones—sons of maids and prostitutes—are everywhere in the city, fending for themselves, leaving room at home for younger ones. These first few days in Colombia, they have given Andrés a strange feeling, thoughts of Marcia again, and how his parents sent her away pregnant. Not of Marcia so much, but of the child. It could be any of these boys. When they thrust their hard, dirty palms before him, he searches their faces for some resemblance to her, or to himself, and always seems to find it. Then a feeling so painful comes over him that he cannot even stop to hand them some coins before he walks away angrily.

He walks quickly past them now, holding Susan on his shoulder above their grasping hands. She strains at his arms as he walks, until he puts her down and lets her go scampering toward the steps of the church. I love to see my pretty daughter run so boldly! I would have chosen a dark Colombian son, but I love my serious, bespectacled little boy and this golden daughter even more. Like me, they belong to two countries—with the gringa blondness of their mother, and the long cheeks and Indian eyes of the Alvarez. And their skin pale gold.

He quickens his gait to match Susita's little leaps up the steps. "Come, Papá," she invited, reaching up for his hand.

"Venga," he corrects her. "Tienes que hablar español, m'hijita. You must learn to speak Spanish."

"I do, Papa, I speak Spanish," says David.

"Of course you do," says his father. "Claro que sí!"

"What, Papa?" Susita does not look up, she is concentrating on the ascent to each new step. "Ven-ga." Right foot, left foot. "Ven-ga." They are at the top of the stairs, and he stops with her to wait for Francisca and Laura.

The church in front of them is whitewashed stucco, beautifully cared for. He likes to see things kept clean like this. The tiles of the roof hang over the edge of the walls above him, and he sees a small bird fly out from one of them. They enter through a great carved doorway and find that the main aisle is taken up by a family of supplicants.

A fat, shabbily dressed woman is in front, walking forward on her knees. Her four children all kneel behind her, each of them carrying a lighted candle and inching forward slowly on bony knees. The smallest is no bigger than Susita, and the candle in his hand wobbles from side to side, flickering dangerously. Andrés hopes Laura won't notice, but knows by the way she glances at him that she already has. He feels very protective of his country suddenly, and can't bear her American judgments.

"That little boy may set fire to himself!" she whispers. "Why do they allow it?"

She is right, of course. The child with the candle makes him wince also, he has become so American. But he will answer like a Colombian. "His father is probably dying," he whispers sternly. "They are asking God to save their father."

"With a human sacrifice?"

He ignores her. He did not know the sharpness of her tongue before he married her. She seemed to be all sweetness, to be a perfect wife. Mostly she still tries to be, but that sharpness will come and prove her false, again and again.

David is tugging at his hand. "I want one! I want one of those!" he points to the candle in the little boys hands."

"Me too!" says Susan.

"Not now." Andrés shrugs, flashes a sardonic glance at Laura. Okay, you win.

"This way," says Francisca. "I show you my *Cristo*, Laura." She leads them over the shining tile floor and up to the nearest side aisle, until they come to some steps behind the altar. Andrés remembers it all clearly as he walks behind the women, though he has not thought of this church in years. Yes, there is the *Cristo* in the glass coffin, resting on a little balcony behind the altar. They climb up to it and stand around the sparkling glass, with the too-realistic *corpus-Christi* inside.

"Look, Laura," Francisca says. "A miracle. The *Cristo* is weeping."

"But it can't be!" Laura stares at it more closely, then turns to Andrés. "It is made of glass, isn't it? The tear on his cheek?"

For an atheist, my wife is very impressionable! He does not answer her, but stares at the enameled cheek with its one glass tear below the right eye. I was twelve and Francisca fifteen when she first told me the same thing. Did she really believe it herself? She gave me a fright that sent me to confession for many months afterward. Only when Carlitos told me it was glass did I realize the trickery. Not that I object to trickery, when it brings people to God. But does Francisca really believe in the tear? And if the tear is not glass, but real, then is not the blood dripping from the thorns on the forehead real blood, and the blood on the palms also? Why does Francisca speak only of the tear?

Laura asks again, insistently. "It isn't a real miracle, is it Andrés?"

"No one knows," he says. Perhaps she might be converted yet. By their Colombian churches and their statues with tears. Perhaps even an intellectual gringa can know God here—at least, one who is half-crazy, writing mystical messages with a hand she says is not her own. But do *I* know God here? A foolish question.

Francisca is pointing to the walls along the side behind the altar, where dozens of crutches are fastened in a haphazard lattice-work. "Proofs of miracles," she says. Francisca is ardent, she is transformed. He cannot bear to answer any more of Laura's questions. Let Francisca handle them.

"I want to get some air," he tells them. "I'll walk around awhile and meet you in front of the church," he tells the children. "I want to get some pictures." Laura holds onto them as he walks back to the front of the church, brushing against the little priest with the polished forehead who has always been there. The dangling camera bumps against Andrés's knee as he genuflects on the way out.

He takes the path among the life-sized Stations of the Cross, where pilgrims kneel before each statue. Walking quickly past, he pauses only before the replica of the Pieta, where a dark young woman kneels on the ground. She wears a handsome wool suit, a black lace shawl over her head. He once gave such a shawl to Laura, but it is usually wrinkled up in the corner of a drawer, and she is unable to find it whenever he tries to take her to Mass. This woman will get runs in her stockings, kneeling on the rough ground like that. He walks on swiftly. There is something disturbing about so many life-sized Christs in one place. Which one to pray to? Which one has the *real* sacred heart?

The path grows narrower and weedier and leads to the edge of the mountain. Pebbles scrape and roll under his feet as he walks to the edge and observes the steep green fall to the city. He looks down the green slopes, across the eucalyptus trees, to where the buildings begin. First the small huts of the poor, then the old houses from Colonial days, then the modern business buildings scattered among the old. The bull ring shambling, ugly, enduring as the Coliseum of Rome. He would take Laura to see the *corrida,* if only he could rely on her not to take the part of the bull, as Americans always do. He does not need to see it for himself any more. The *toro* and *torero,* they paw and swoop inside him vividly enough, endlessly. Am I the *toro* or the *torero,* he used to ask himself as a boy. He never knew.

In the center of the city, the big buildings. The banks. Of course the banks; tall and modern, bold. The Tequendama Hotel, American of course. But I am American now.

Traded my country for the land of golden opportunity, for double the salary, for a blond wife and two children, for the comfort of not being murdered on a weekend in the country. My country, home of La Violencia.

The news would seep into his American life now and then, reminding him. "Colombian Bus Attacked by Bandits. Twenty-four People Beheaded and Mutilated." Political violence turned into butchery for the hell of it, banditry as a way of life. And the politicians played their games and ignored the meaning of it all, the underneath meaning of terrible inequality. But what could he have done about it, even if he had stayed? He is only one man.

His eyes scan the city. Between the new buildings are the old, streets and streets of the ugly old houses with beautiful Colonial sections showing through here and there. The Plaza de Bolívar; they could be proud of that at least. Bolívar's statue small in the middle of it, the pigeons all around—he can't see them from here, yet his mind adds them, they are so much a part of it. Then the impressive Capitol building. The State greater than the Liberator, as it should be. But as it is? Now the State fumbles on, and no man to equal the murdered Gaitán has appeared in fifteen years. And Bolívar's equal has never come again. The statue and the Capitol reflect the Liberator's modesty and his hope for the State. And there is the Cathedral with the little closed-down ancient church beside it. He loved it best of all before they closed it down. It seemed like the real church, and the Cathedral only an institution.

"Señor Gringo! Do you have a few centavos for us?" The voice is shrill, yet commanding. His heart jumps, his camera falls to the end of its strap. "Señor?"

He looks around at three middle-sized urchins. "What are you doing here?"

"We climb, Señor." The tallest boy, about eleven or twelve, grins at him. They stand blocking his way, the precipice behind him. They are small and undernourished, but one push and he'd lose his balance, fall over the side. They'd want his camera first, though, and that would mean a struggle. They wouldn't dare, unless they hated him enough.

They could hate me. They should. I left them, didn't I? Left them to beg all over Bogotá. The tall one might be my own son, he has the long face, the Alvarez eyes. But so are they all, all the *gamines*—my abandoned sons.

"What can you give us, Señor? Are you tired? Do you want help over to the funicular?" The tone of the tall one, the boy his son's age, is friendly. The other two boys do not speak; they only watch.

Andrés grins at them. He has abandoned them, yet he is a *gamin* himself, as homeless as they are. "No. No, gracias. Here. Take this." He gives them a handful of coins. They could have had his life, but he will not show it. Probably they don't realize it. Probably they do.

CHAPTER 12

Guitars and Windmills

Laura goes for a walk alone. She walks through the chill of a gray afternoon, away from the main part of the city, up a cobblestone hill where the shabby houses are older and prettier. Outside a shop two men sit on the sidewalk on workbenches, making guitars. One is sanding the wood of a new guitar. The other is stringing a finished instrument. The wood is rich, rubbed to a fine glow. The show window is crowded with guitars and amateur sketches of the city, hanging from wires, swaying slightly.

Laura stops to watch the men. Their hands are deft, gentle. Their eyes flash under old felt hats.

Oh if I could buy one of these guitars and learn its music! The men smile at her. "Do you wish a guitar, Señorita?" And if I bought one—do your guitars know the secret songs of the men of Colombia, of men anywhere, so I can understand my husband? Are there songs for women hidden in them? Do your guitars strum how to live in the Andean mist without being sad?

They pause in their work, continuing to smile at her. She looks in her purse, but there is not enough money. "I will be back," she tells them. "I have a little money saved at home." There is something hopeful and thrilling about seeing these guitars being made, actually being made on this cobblestone hill with its small white shops and tile-roofed houses. The street of the guitar-makers.

"I will be back," she tells them again. "Save me a good one!"

"Señorita, we will!" they laugh.

On the way down the hill she runs and skips a little. At a corner, an old woman sits on the pavement, selling toy windmills. She wears a fedora above her round, wrinkled face with its high cheekbones, black button eyes. A tall rack of windmills twirls merrily over her head, but the woman herself is stoic, enduring the air of a windless place.

"May I take your picture?" Laura asks. The woman nods soberly. Laura looks through the camera at the merry windmills, the somber face. Is that me? Is that me with the sad heart and the joyous wind unnoticed, just above my head? She buys windmills for Susan and David, and one for Concha's Miguel, and walks the rest of the way home with windmills twirling. For half a block she holds them over her head, feeling the wind. Sailing.

CHAPTER 13

Francisca and Laura

The beggar holds out his stub of an arm, but it only frightens Laura. Nor is there hand to drop the money in. She nearly trips over phantom legs of a legless girl. Perfect eyes imploring. Why am I here? Oh why am I here, the girl and Laura cry out to each other, and Laura stumbles on. She has not given.

She hates downtown Bogotá. Francisca is half a block ahead of her now, carrying Susan over her shoulder. Glimpses of Susan's little face now and then, looking back anxiously for Laura, who struggles on with David pulling at her hand. It is easy to keep them in sight, Francisca is so tall—taller than most men here. Only the American men and that stilt man advertising a movie seem taller. But she moves so fast Laura and David can't keep up. Begging hands, jostling shoulders hold them back. And it makes her nervous, holding onto her little boy, to see her baby disappearing into the strangeness of the crowd.

Francisca frightens me too, Laura thinks. She seems half-mad, and evil-tempered—yet kind, kinder than the others. I don't know what she may do next, or what she wants from me. But I am a coward, to hand my child to her whenever she insists. And Andrés won't help. Be easy, he says. Try to get along with my family. Then he goes off to his microfilming and leaves me at home with them. It's easiest when the little cousins are running around the cold hotel, giggling and spying with each other, making things brighter. But the coldness, the grayness are always there. And Francisca always on the edge of violence; every day new explosions of anger with the servants, or loud arguments with Pilar and Elena. Only with poor Tía Marta in that dark room, does she seem at peace. But to us Francisca is kind, if not peaceful: "Do you like to go to the museum with me?" "Do you like a cup of coffee?" "Speak only English, please, I no like to speak Spanish." This with her big, too-generous, charming smile. At first she helped my loneliness and I was touched. But now it begins to frighten me, this intensity of kindness, this intensity of something desperate underneath. It is like the automatic writing, the terror I have felt over that—the gift of love and the threat of death (you will die in Colombia, do not go). It is as if all that is in Francisca, as if she is the nucleus and the secret, and—how terrifying that is!

Laura stumbles over the pot-holed pavement now and dodges the streams of urine that trickle from the sides of marble buildings to dirty curbside. She has lost sight of Francisca and Susan in the crowd ahead. Despair wells up. Why am I here as a wife, an in-law, half a prisoner, when I might have been a tourist, a detached observer? This forced intimacy with strangers—not even my strangers, but his. His strangers. And we are strangers to each other, too. Everything is foreign, not just the country. Everything. My life is foreign to me.

Laura's eyes meet those of a tiny boy, face covered with dust and tear-streaked. His feet are bound in rags for shoes, and he sits bare-bottomed on the dirty sidewalk, leaning against the marble facade of a bank. He is putting his penis in and taking it out of a broken toy car. Learning to be a machine, is that it, so young? David is pulling at her hand again, wanting to stop, wanting to see.

If I were a tourist, I wouldn't see this, my child wouldn't see this. I would be laughingly going in and out of an American hotel with my American husband. We would see the

Tequendama Falls and look at emeralds in store windows, but not this. We would not notice death in children's eyes. If I were a tourist, I would not even come here!

Sound of screeching brakes at the corner ahead. Laura hears Francisca's voice raised in angry Spanish. "Bruto! Tonto!" Pushing, dodging desperately, holding tight to David, she reaches the corner, finds Francisca exchanging insults with a taxi driver who almost hit her—and Susan! Laura forces her way through the people who stand laughing at the uproar, and, letting go of David, she puts her arms around her baby, pulling her away from Francisca. Susan's face is pale beside her blonde curls, and she is stiff with fright, refusing to nestle her cheek against Laura's shoulder. David pulls at her skirt. "Mommy! Mom!"

The taxi driver slams his door and drives away triumphantly.

"No importa, Francisca," Laura says. "Let's go home now."

Francisca, with no way to vent her anger, begins to walk beside them. Her large, passionate features are grim, and the blunt ends of her straight black hair swing against her cheeks. The poufed hairdo she wore for their arrival deteriorated long ago.

"I take Susan now," she insists, reaching out for the little girl. Bogotá's crowded streets frighten Susan, and she refuses to walk in them. Andrés says she is too old for a stroller. Besides, they can't afford one. "Why don't you walk like your brother?" they all ask her, but Susan only clings tighter and if they put her down to make her walk, she just sits on the hard cement and refuses to move.

"No, gracias." Laura shifts Susan to the opposite hip and holds on tight again to David's hand. He is tugging, pulling, as if he wants to run away. "It's okay, Davy, it's okay," she tells him. Her arms ache and she trembles with anger at Francisca, at the driver, at Andrés. If only I had come here before I married him! (Do not go to Colombia, you will die in Colombia do not go. Or my children! Perhaps it meant my children!)

"Very well." Francisca relents and begins threading through the crowds ahead of them again. Laura pushes past the beggars and lottery vendors as best she can, and eventually catches up with Francisca outside the hotel.

The street where the Hotel Del Libertador stands is lined with small bars and grimy delicatessens along the ground level, with hotels and small apartments converted from the upper stories of neglected Colonial buildings. Now, shivering in the chilly air, Laura, still holding Susan, stands beside Francisca outside the hotel entrance. She glances up at the twin green mountains, Monserrate and Guadalupe, overlooking the city. Green escape from city death, city gray. She looks up there often, ever since the day Francisca took them to see the church on Monserrate, with its weeping Christ and its miracles. "Look at the crutches on the walls!" Francisca said then, as if her own crutch were among them. A miracle could change a life. Many lives. What would I hang on the wall if the weeping Christ changed my life? A bagful of little crutches, all the false images I live by? Where is the gift of love, I wonder. And what is it?

Francisca bangs on the door, impatient for the porter to let them in. The door is kept locked at all times because of thefts, though everyone knows it is useless: the porter himself is the thief. Hilario is his name, but he never smiles. Scowling now, he lets them in. Francisca rushes angrily up the stairs, and Laura with Susan strains up the steps behind her, her arms aching. She catches up with Francisca at the door of her room. "Thank you for the walk." Hypocrisy! You might have killed my baby, and you frightened my little boy. And you are my husband's sister. "Thank you."

Francisca nods, then points to a newspaper clipping taped to her door. "Look. The schedule for Independence week. I take you to all the events, the big parade. It is Colombia's happiest time." She leans down to the children. "A parade, David! A parade, Susita!" She straightens again and looks at Laura intently with her fierce brown eyes. "Then soon—maybe you take me to parades in the United States."

"Maybe," says Laura cautiously. Andrés has told Francisca again and again that Laura has no connections, no friends in high places, no way to get a new visa for someone who was sent out of the country "officially" crazy. Still to Francisca she is a kind of mythical person, a gringa, blessed with special privileges and powers. Still Francisca thinks Laura can make everything right again, recover the jewels and the lost dreams. Dreams so desperate or bright she betrayed this great pride of hers to try to be a servant. Francisca, who shouts at the maids as if she were born a queen.

Francisca is staring at her. "Your purse!" she says. "You left it open in the street.".

Laura looks down to see her bag unsnapped and gaping open. "But I didn't!"

"Mommy, I tried to tell you," says David, "But you didn't listen!"

"We told you not to hang it over the arm like that," Francisca scolds. "Now you are robbed, that is certain. You must carry it close to your body and hold on tight, like this." She clutches her own bag dramatically to her bosom.

Laura dumps all the contents of her bag on the dull parquet floor and scrambles through them anxiously. Susan, thinking it is a game, stoops beside her, playing with the jumble of objects. "Mommy's stuff!" she laughs. David laughs and joins in with her.

"My wallet is gone!" Laura cries. "All my money and the room key were in it." Hastily, she snatches the thin little notebook-diary from Susan and puts it in the bag again. Susan picks up her lipstick and pulls it open.

"Of course," says Francisca. "We told you that will happen. Bogotá is a city of thieves. Now you will have to ask my mother for a new key. Was it much money?" she adds, more sympathetically. "Let me help you."

She squats on the floor and gently helps Susan close the lipstick and put the other things back in Laura's bag. "Gracias á Díos, your passport is here."

"Thank you," Laura says. "I guess I'll go for another key." But she is afraid to get up from the floor and face her mother-in-law. Her guitar money was in the wallet, the little bit of her own money that she had. She was going to go back today to buy that guitar for herself and learn to make music on it, Colombian folk songs like the ones she hears in, the bar below their room. The music was going to make a link between her and Colombia, between her and Andrés.

"My guitar money is gone," Laura says.

"Lastima! What a shame," Francisca sympathizes. "And you like the guitars so much." She smiles suddenly. "But when you go back to America and I come to see you there, I will bring you one. It will be all right."

Laura smiles sadly. The trip to the United States again. Can't she see I'm a prisoner and a blunderer, not a performer of miracles? Her brother's introvert wife, not a sleek tourist with matching luggage and money to buy emeralds? But Francisca is not asking now—she is only being kind.

"Thank you." Laura pulls herself off the floor and gathers up the children, taking their hands. "Let's go see Abuela."

"Abayla?" says Susan.

"Abu-ayla," David corrects her.

"That's right, Davy," she says. "Yes, you know Abuela, Susan. That's how you say Grandma here. Like Grandma in Arizona."

"Abayla not Gramma." Susan shakes her head. She still likes Luisa, the plump, friendly cook, better than her stern grandmother. Both children do, and Miguel as well. They are always welcome in her kitchen, always given something to help with, a pot to stir or some pans to stack up. "May you sleep with the angels," Luisa tells them each night in her deep, warm voice, just before they leave the dining room. "Qué duerma con los angeles." And gives them hugs, and goodnight treats. No, Pilar is not like that.

CHAPTER 14

Pilar

Pilar has divided the huge parlor of the Colonial house into two rooms, a small hotel lobby and her own large bedroom. The plain office partition and plywood door are in awkward contrast to the high, ornate ceiling, which the partition does not attempt to reach. Laura taps on the door.

"Doña Pilar," she calls. A soap opera is proceeding in Spanish on Pilar's ancient radio. Husky voices, full of static, exude sentimentality. A passionate, deep-voiced woman and a sad, earnest man questioning each other, questioning and weeping as the world turns. Pilar does not answer until the scene ends.

"Piña para la niña," shouts the announcer in a static-filled base. "Aliño para el niño, y Glama para la Dama. . ."

When the commercial begins, Pilar opens the door to Laura. "Come in." She turns the radio down to a low buzz and sits on the bed beside it. She is a sharp-featured woman, whose hooked nose must have kept her from being a conventional beauty, even when she was young. Yet the misty photograph that hangs over the bed shows an attractive, romantic girl of half a century earlier, with a strong nose, yes, but posing under a lace drapery and holding a white lily. The photographer must have stuck it in the hands of all the girls who came to him, so he would not have to stay long under the black cloth to get that stylish dreamy quality. Was the lily real? And what about the dreaminess, what about the dreams?

"Lo siento mucho. Doña Pilar," Laura begins. It is painful summoning her Spanish for this unfriendly ear. "I am sorry, but I lost my key. My wallet was stolen in the market."

"Hmmp!" Pilar grunts angrily, shaking her head and swinging her index finger in a scolding arc, like a windshield wiper. "No puedo. I cannot give you another key. This is the second one you have lost."

"But the children are very tired. Where can they sleep?" Laura pleads.

"No puedo," insists Pilar. "No puedo."

Francisca knocks on the door. "Give me the key, Mamá," she says. "I will let them in and return it to you."

"Very well." Relenting, Pilar hobbles over to the fat wardrobe with a huge portrait of Pope Pius XII hanging above it. She takes a key from her apron and opens the wardrobe door, where the room keys hang on hooks, three rows of them.

"Here." She gives the key to Laura. "I would come," she says, suddenly gentle. "But my feet hurt so much. I have to walk all day and they are very tired."

"I'm sorry about your feet," says Laura. "Thank you for the key."

"And how are my little grandchildren?" Pilar collects a shy kiss from David, then turns to Susan. "No hablas español?" Susan shakes her head. "Un beso, pues. A kiss for your old grandmother."

"OK," says Susan, after Laura has given her a hopeful push. She allows herself to be swung up, and puts a kiss on the old woman's cheek, which looks so hard and yet is very soft. Laura remembers her surprise at that when she kissed Pilar at the airport.

Pilar chuckles, putting Susan down, clapping her bottom. "Now go on," she says. "This is my only time to rest, and I am an old woman. But Francisca, you return the key at once."

Francisca comes back to Laura's room after returning the key. "Do you want to hear the story of Mamá's first marriage?" she asks. "In Spanish?"

"Sí," says Laura. Susan is already napping on one bed, and even David has fallen asleep on his father's bed. Laura gives Francisca the only chair, then settles on the nearest bed to listen. She has heard the story from Andrés, of course, for this is the family's romantic legend. But Francisca will tell it in a different way, a woman's way. And she has just been thinking of that misty photograph. Pilar in white, a lily in her hand.

"I am going to tell you just the way it was," says Francisca. Her eyes are gleaming with excitement, her mouth full of storytelling confidence.

CHAPTER 15

Pilar's First Marriage

Carlos lay in bed and she sat beside him, bent over him. Her knees were wet underneath, at the backs they were wet, her dress smelled. His breaths were broken seeds, broken little birds that had no feathers yet and fell out of their nests. The heat was crawling over her, over him. She waved a woven funeral fan to cool his face.

"Marry me," he pleaded. "Now . . ."

"I will," she said. "But tomorrow. We will have a true marriage. I will wear white." (And with roses! She had roses!)

"Yes," he smiled faintly. So handsome a face, so very handsome and sensitive. Like a wounded bullfighter, brave and fainting away, pale and handsome. (He was not our father but our uncle, Francisca whispers. He was very very handsome!) Once he had pulled her along beside him, running to the beach to see a rainstorm out over the ocean, pencil lines of rain straight down, straight down from black sky to sea. Once he had pulled her along to see that, while she hung back laughing, and his strong hand pulled her.

Francisco Pablo stood outside the room waiting for her. Cold and troubled. Warm and troubled. "What did he want?"

"We are going to be married," she answered. (White roses!)

"But he is dying!"

"It doesn't matter. I love him. You do not have to do anything. Nobody has to. I will see the priest myself. I will arrange it all myself." So little time to arrange the white dress. to make it beautiful enough, the ordinary Sunday dress. And trouble with the priest, convincing him. She trembled to go, to make joy for Carlos.

"You are foolish," Francisco said, but he walked away. He was thinking about the Liberator and the Revolution. He was thinking about the wars of Liberation. A dying brother took his breath out, made his books smell old, old, made his heart smell of old books. (*He* was our father! I was named for him and his dust of books. If Carlos had lived . . .) He went away thinking of death, but he also thought of roses. She could at least have roses, white roses. He was glad she was still a virgin when his brother died. He wept for Carlos when he died, everyone wept. But it was good she was still a virgin, a virgin widow, almost a saint.

CHAPTER 16

Francisca's Elopement

"And now," says Francisca, "I have to tell you *my* love story. It is sadder than our mother's because there is no wedding in it. No roses."

Enrique was a schoolteacher, a naturalist, small and thin and quick. He asked me to come with him into the jungle. We would collect my country's beautiful creatures and strange creatures and bring them back to the university. They would be pleased and offer him a place, a distinguished position.

"When they see the wonderful collection I bring, they will marvel!" He was very sure. He liked to tell me how sure he was, when he came with my cousin to visit us. "All the creatures crawl into my boxes, into my bags. I sing, and they come!" He used to say that and sing a little song, like a snake charmer. We talked in the patio alone about Colombia's beauty, the green skin, green veins. I wanted to go with him into her secret places and bring back what I feel in here, inside me. The mysteries. I have seen the little gold frogs in the museum and I knew about their deadly poison. And I saw the giant worms on ancient pots, carved before God came to our land, before the priests. "Yes," I said to him. I loved him so much I even said "querido" to him. "Yes, querido, I will come with you."

He said he would not have asked any other woman. "Women are frail and full of fear," he said. "But you—" He was kissing me then, kissing my throat and my eyes. "You are very strong," he said. "You are strong, muñeca, my big doll, Francisca." And I was, I was strong for him.

We travelled with no one but ourselves, and many bags to carry. Boys would help us at the village places, but mostly I carried my load like a man. The specimen boxes were tied with rope, and we dragged them with us onto the train and then into the boat as we went down the river, On the first night, we had already entered the secret world. Hammocks were hung between buildings, across the little street of the village we came to. Three white men lay there with goatskin bags of aguardiente, like baby bottles in their arms. Enrique paid them to let us use one hut alone, and we hung our hammocks in it.

When he climbed into my hammock, sprang into it so suddenly and shocked my soul, the beams it hung from creaked, and I thought it would fall. I felt myself falling away, away—as if the length of Tequendama. I began to struggle, but he put his knuckles gently into my mouth and let me gnaw at them, uselessly, and he kissed my eyes and my neck. And with his other hand—and his knuckles slid gently in my mouth until 1 began to suck at them and kiss them, and then mouth came where his hand had been, and his lips pressed and pressed and the hammock swayed. I loved him, but I wanted to die, to die of shame. For I knew this would happen, and I had come without marriage be-cause I wanted him so much. And yet I did not want it, no I didn't. Sweet Virgin forgive me, I didn't want it. I thought he would see how strong and helpful Francisca is, and he would say yes, you should be my wife, you should be with me in all my work and all my life.

We slept awhile together, tangled in the ropes of the hammock. His light body was sweet to me, it lay upon me like the bough of a tree. I did not mind the terrible heat and this wet body against mine. It was as if a green tree of the mountain air, and not of the jungle, lay on my soul. Still, inside I knew the truth, and I wept.

When I woke, he was sleeping in the other hammock. and I could feel the tears dried on my face, and the moisture dried on my legs. From the doorway, the Indian he had talked to yesterday looked straight at me. He held up two giant worms, three feet long. The same as on the ancient pots! "How much he pay?"

I called in fear and joy, "Enrique! Enrique!" He woke up at once. He was always so quick, so ready. He smiled at the Indian. One worm was three and a half feet long—dark and ridged, just like the little earthworms. But big, very thick and black, like a snake. Enrique took it gladly in his hands.

"Yes, yes," he said. "Tell your friends I want more. I will pay them for more!" They were the same worms on the ancient pots, they were the secret of the earth, the creatures who made the jungle earth so sweet and beautiful. But they dangled ugly in front of me, and he laughed at me for being afraid. "Where is my brave Francisca?" And so I held them, their ridged black forms, and felt how they were still alive, still had the power in them to enter the Colombian earth they loved. But I was afraid and sick inside.

"When can we look for the golden frogs?"

"Soon," he said. And we went on horseback that day, finding Indians who could bring us frogs, green, red, and black, even the black-and-gold. All of them could kill us with their poison. The poison from one frog could tip the arrows of many Indians with poison for their enemy. But I thought of the gold jewel frogs in the museums and I knew the ancient Indians had not loved them for their poison but for some other secret. The living gold frogs, they would teach me something.

But I have not learned the secret yet, though I have been studying the myths and telling the ancient stories in my head. I am still waiting. All I received in that jungle was the poison, when Enrique told me we could never marry. The poison went through me so fast that the world almost died. It is still inside me now, it still burns. That is why I have to go back, go back to America and find a new life, Laura. I have to leave those poison frogs behind!

CHAPTER 17

Carmen the Bird Girl

Laura stirs the lump of sugar in her demitasse, playing idly with the little spoon. Oh to be a lady and have a set of tiny cups and spoons like this to play dolls with. (But I will never be a lady, though Andrés may wish it with all his heart.) What are they talking about now? I don't want to be dolls with them.

She nods now and then, not really trying to listen. She and Andrés and the children have been in Bogotá three weeks now, but she can still shut off her college Spanish when she likes, and not hear anything. There have been only a few formal visits like this, to friends of his family, but still they are too many. Señor Martinez and Andrés are doing most of the talking just now. The wife, plump in her tight black dress and cherry colored shawl, watches over things in a hungry way, as if their eating will feed her hunger. The children are at the hotel with Rosa watching them. How she wishes she could have stayed there too!

Underneath the table, the heavy Spanish table by the wall, someone looks at Laura. Little round face and clever, knowing eyes. Semi smile floating. A person crouching there. Who are you, the eyes are asking.

Who are *you*?

I see you.

Yes, I see you too. Who are you?

Help me!

Sharp, intelligent little face, kindred to my own. I am crouching under a table too. I don't know why I'm here, or what this life is. I married a stranger, a foreigner, and now the foreigner is me. Crouching under a table, just like you. But who are you?

"Carmen! Why are you hiding there, you naughty?" Señora Martinez nudges her husband. "Look at her! Spying again!"

He shrugs. "Send her back, then. She gives me the creeps, anyway."

"No. She is intelligent, pobrecita. Poor little thing!" She turns to Laura and Andrés. "She will never get any bigger! I let her do a little work and stay here with us. Not much good for work—I had a nine-year-old maid who could do more work in a day—but very intelligent! Come out of there. Carmen!"

Two, three steps forward. Semi smile hovering. Help me!

"See, look how tiny she is!" Round little pillow of a body, spindly arms and legs. Shivering in the sleeveless white shift. I know those eyes. No doll's face this. Who are you?

"Say something, Carmen." The eyes watch cleverly. The smile flaps its wings a few times; gone.

"All right, then. Go tell Maria to give you some work. Go on." A kind of bowlegged dignity, as she turns and walks away. Now we will be dolls again. Now we will stir more sugar lumps into the ugly brew. Señora Martinez pulls the cherry colored shawl around plump shoulders, bends forward smiling, and lifts the pot. Will-you-won't-you have another cup my dear?

"Andrés," says Laura on the way home. "She was cold in there. I want to give her one of Susan's sweaters."

"I know," he says. "But you can't. They will be offended."

"Why?"

"They will think you are insulting them, that they don't take proper care of her." Her once-revolutionary husband, talking of propriety! She thinks sadly of how, when she met him, he used to dream aloud of overthrowing the dictator who ruled his country then, and how she wanted to be a part of the adventure. But she was just a foolish girl then, no more ready for a real revolution than he was. No, he was readier than she. And now they are equals, perhaps, in compassion, in sorrow over poverty, over complacent middle-class charity in the form of making servants out of little girls—except that Andrés is embarrassed and avoiding the facts. "Hiring little girls as maids saves them from prostitution," someone told her charitably at dinner last week. But Andrés is caught in proprieties just now, and Laura is impatient. Why should he care if they offend his mother's friends for the sake of kindness?

"Let them be offended!" she insists.

"No. They are old friends of my family." Sadly, he looks away.

But she will do it anyway. She will play tea party again. Francisca is a good conspirator, lonely and half-mad. Though Laura is still frightened of her, Francisca is her only friend.

"Yes," she says at once, when Laura suggests her plan. "Pobrecita. I will take you." Though Francisca, in her desperate isolation, shouts and threatens the maids, she cares about the poor more than anyone else seems to. She weeps for them, and puts newspaper stories about them on her wall. "We will take flowers to make the Señora happy," she says. "I will take care of everything."

Stirring the little cup again, pleased to have rough-hewn Francisca here. She too will never be a lady, though her coarse hair is poufed and teased again by a stupid hair-dresser. When she eloped to the jungle with her natural-ist lover, her hair was not poufed—she was just dreaming Francisca. Like Laura, she does not play dolls very well. She beams encouragement now, while Laura struggles with courtesies. Tall gladiolas with poufed and awkward hairdos nod, conspiratorial, from Carmen's table by the wall.

"Where is that little girl. Carmen?" Laura asks at last.

"Ah, Carmen!" Señora Martinez smiles. "Yes, isn't she interesting? Some kind of disease she had as a baby. Some deficiency in her diet. But she amazes me—so intelligent!"

"How do you know she is intelligent?" This woman is strange, too. She seems complacent, and yet those clever eyes of Carmen's have reached her. I can tell she is affected; but she isn't used to being reached.

"How is she intelligent?" Señora Martinez hugs her arms in the cherry shawl and answers slowly, enjoying. Enjoying being astute enough to discover intelligence. "Well—she is always spying—trying to learn things. She has never been to school, and yet she has taught herself to read. I caught her with little Jorge's books one day."

"Did you send her to school then?" Of course not. Andrés would be angry. Don't prick at their conscience; leave them alone. Forget all this—how the cook found her somewhere in those slums at the foot of Monserrate and brought her home one night because she felt sorry for her.

Just let me give her this sweater, then let us get away from here. Are you going to be offended? "Since I was coming by, Señora, I thought I'd bring this little sweater for her. Susan has too many, and this one is too big for her." Are you going to be offended?

Only a little. "Certainly. I will send for her." The smile a little strained, but it's all right. Bless Francisca for thinking of flowers!

The clever, searching eyes again. Help me! No semi smile, no demi smile hovering. How stupid I am. How can I know you, here in the dollhouse? Laura holds out the sweater, the pretty blue one her sister made. Pearly buttons in the shape of butterflies, little psyche souls. What a thing, to have this tiny body and the wisdom in those eyes. What do you think? What do you know? To be treated like a toy, and have this electrifying soul.

Carmen tries the sweater on. Nimble little fingers button it, then linger over pearly butterflies. The eyes look up eagerly. Smile flaps its wings a moment. Then gone. What is going to happen to me? Is this all you can do? "Gracias, Señora." High, piping voice, but not a doll's voice. It has an edge, a sharpness. "Francisca!" Laura turns to her excitedly, trying Francisca's English. "Do you think she would let us take Carmen to babysit for the children when we go to the park? Or at the house? As a favor to us, tell her. Could you ask her?"

"What Andrés will say? And my Mamá?" But Francisca slowly smiles her broad, unladylike smile. Her madwoman's wild grin. And Laura loves her for it.

CHAPTER 18

Aviary Dreams

Twice a week now, Laura "borrows" Carmen as a babysitter for David and Susan. Most of the time she stays with them too, for she is alone while Andrés is working anyway, and as they play, she teaches Carmen everything she can. "Do not tell the Señora," she says. "This is your secret school." She tries to explain that she does not like to be devious, but that this is a special case, involving the growth of a special person. Carmen nods eagerly and Francisca laughs. For she comes too, proud teacher and translator. For all of them, Carmen's lessons give some sense of hope, of meaning, maybe even love.

Carmen loves birds. Gradually Laura has been learning this, seeing how she puts her head to one side and listens sometimes when there are birds nearby, or watches them in flight. "What do you want most?" she asks Carmen idly one day, as the five of them picnic on the ugly, shabby grass in the park. For some reason, the parks are very ugly here. People in dark ruanas wander sadly on the paths; children sometimes manage to laugh or shout. The best moments are at noon, when wives bring their husbands complete hot lunches in steaming metal pans stacked in tiers and fastened together. Laura would almost like to be a woman who is mistress of such clever pans, the brief warmth and flavor of some workman's midday. It is what Andrés would like, she thinks. But he has had a quick, dark lunch with them and gone back to his microfilm. They linger with books and

David and Susan's toy airplanes, which they send on brief, doomed flights, then scamper after.

"What do you want most?" Laura asks Carmen, this day.

"To grow," comes the answer. Oh yes, to grow. Look at us, none of us able to grow. Laura with her Latin dreams turned into disappointment, Francisca with her lost jungle love, and Carmen with no promises at all.

Now Carmen cries out fiercely in her new English, "To grow!" She points to the row of flower pots with a growing flower on the page of the language book; to the graduated oak trees; to the picture of a little chick getting bigger and bigger.

"But dear Carmen, you can't grow much bigger in the body. You won't be grandissima, not ever." Laura turns a page in another book, Susan's *Mother Goose,* and shows her the tiny nut tree with its silver nutmeg and golden pear.

> I had a little nut tree, nothing would it bear
> But a silver nutmeg, and a golden pear.
> The King of Spain's daughter came to visit me
> And all was because of my little nut tree.

"You will be a little tree like this, a precious one," she pleads. With silver fruit and gold. Carmen looks with eyes of terror and runs across the grass to the tangle of weird trees with contorted, low-hanging branches. She jumps into one like a small monkey and begins screaming, keening, wailing. Laura watches, not daring to move.

"Then let me be a bird!" Carmen cries out in Spanish, climbing with fierce energy. Across the patchy grass, Laura can see her eyes gleaming.

"Stupid!" Francisca shouts. "Shall I come there and beat you?" Susan drops her airplane and runs laughingly to the bottom of the tree.

"I will fly!" Carmen answers. She struggles upward in intricate branches, calling down in her piercing voice. "You leave me alone! *Let* me be a bird!" Susan stands below, round cheeked and wondering, looking up. David, who is nearly as big as Carmen, begins to climb after her. "Oh, Davy!" Laura laughs. "But don't go too high, please!"

Suddenly she remembers something.

"Come down, Davy," she calls softly, walking toward the tree. "Come down, Carmen! I was wrong about growing. I was stupid! There are many ways to grow, and many ways to fly. You have made me remember something wonderful, and now I know what we can do. It will make us all happy! Will you come if I find the book about the bird girl for you? There is really such a book!"

Astonished eyes look down; the sharp little smile appears. "The bird girl?"

David has already landed on the ground, with an assured, boyish thump. "A book?" he says.

Green Mansions. Andrés will find it in the library for her. Oh blessed escape! Conjunction of our dreams. Didn't I expect to be some grand combination of Rima the bird girl and Evita Peron? Weekends I would spend in the jungle, in "that immense aerial palace hung with dim drapery" of leaves, friend of all the forest creatures, enchantress of my vagabond love (who might or might not resemble Andrés). Weekdays, I would return to the city, assisting my husband, the great Revolutionist, in his work of liberating the masses. (They would adore me.)

And Francisca has had dreams too. She comes to listen now, whenever they read together. "I know about green mansions," she says. "I have been there, no? I have had the real adventure!"

"Yes," says Laura. They sit sometimes in one gray room of the house, sometimes in another. Carmen is the pure new dreamer, and gives herself wholly to the joy of it. Laura reads in English, then translates. All the children sit on the floor, listening in two languages. But Carmen thinks she has heard it in the secret language that can't be translated:

> "Why do you not answer me?—speak to me—speak to me, like this!" And turning a little more towards me, and glancing at me

with eyes that had all at once changed, losing their clouded expression for one of exquisite tenderness, from her lips came a succession of those mysterious sounds which had first attracted me to her, swift and low and birdlike, yet with something so much higher and more soul-penetrating than any bird- music . . . . To me they would always be inarticulate sounds, affecting me like a tender spiritual music—a language without words, suggesting more than words to the soul.

"That is *my* language," says Carmen. And what does it matter if she's only pretending, Laura thinks. For in a sense it's true. And the three of them, the woman who is half-mad and the woman who is afraid she is half-mad, and the girl whose body will not grow—and maybe even the little children too—are beginning to realize that like Rima they each have their own language no one else can listen to. But they begin to hear one another now and then by making room for soft, bird-sounding silences.

"Now I know what I want," says Carmen one day. "I want to live with the birds." Laura hears her say it. Francisca hears it. Francisca, almost six feet tall and condor-like, straining to understand the smallness of Carmen. "I want to live with the birds, I want my own little sky, I want my own little forests, and the birds to live with me!"

Francisca hears, but gives up trying to know this language. She laughs scornfully. "Maybe she will fly away on the condor's back!"

Carmen gives her a look of terror. "Not the death bird!" she cries. "The sweet birds. The gentle ones."

"Condor is not the death bird," says Francisca. "It is symbol of our country. Giant heart, giant wings!" But Carmen will not consider condors.

Laura begins to think of possibilities. Schemes of aviaries, Carmen under a little aviary sky, tending the birds. Could it be made to happen? And she has to reckon with the ending of *Green Mansions,* which they will come to very soon. She had forgotten how Rima is burned to death in her tree by those who fear her strangeness, how she never reached her own people, the ones who spoke her language.

No, Carmen would despair if she heard that ending. She has become Rima. And the younger children must not hear such an ending either! I must commit the double sin, rewriting life and art at once. Schemes of aviaries, dreams of Carmen among the birds, Rima finding her people at last, under opalescent rainbow dome, Carmen's own dream sky. In the fairy tale, Thumbelina flew away on the back of a gentle bird. Why not Carmen the bird girl, somehow? Laura searches for a way to tell it in the secret language, for then it might all come true.

CHAPTER 19

Concha Lying In—and In—

Concha has had her baby, a little boy, two weeks ago. She has taken Carmen away from Laura and put her to work fetching clean diapers, rinsing soiled ones, and performing dozens of little services while she lies in bed. At the same time. Concha has committed herself to the improvement of Laura.

"Let me teach you how to paint your nails," she says. Laura gives in, but she is feeling angry. She has never painted her nails; she has always thought it barbarous. She sits on a hardback chair next to Concha's bed, for Concha makes the most of childbirth—has a real, old-fashioned "lying in." Laura can see she has no intention of getting dressed for another week or two, at least, and she laughs to herself over this.

Concha briskly takes Laura's hand and shows her how to do a proper manicure—how to push her cuticles back, to shape the nails into points, how to apply the plum-colored frosted polish. Ugh! All the while, Laura is watching Carmen, who likes the baby, but hates Concha. She is supposed to rock the cradle just now.

Concha lays one of Laura's hands on the bedspread and picks up the other, while she lectures her also on the wearing of nylons. "You know, only prostitutes go without stockings in the street," she says kindly, in Spanish.

"I didn't realize," says Laura meekly. She can hardly bear the deft touch of the brush on her nails, or the chemical smell of the polish, or Concha's rich voice. She hears the pleasant noises of Miguel and David, playing at cars and trucks in the corridor outside, while Susan sits beside her on the bed.

"Now," says Concha, after a minute of concentration. She sets the second hand on the bedspread, as if it were a newly frosted cake. She picks up the first and blows on it. "Here, wave it in the air," she tells Laura, giving it back to her. "Now it is Susan's turn."

Susan looks up gleefully. "Now me?"

"Sí," says Concha. "We are going to make you beautiful! Don't smudge, Laura," she adds warningly, as Laura ventures to repossess her hands. "Susita, you climb here," she says, patting the bed beside her. Susan is beginning to climb up eagerly, when the baby starts to scream.

Pushing Susan aside. Concha leaps out of the bed. "Carmen! You little pig! What have you done to him?" She slaps Carmen on the side of the head, knocking her over. "Get over there," she screams. "Get over in the corner until I see what you've done." She picks up the baby, searches it and finds a red mark on its little arm, which already looks rounder and plumper than Carmen's. "I knew it," she says to Laura. "Look at this—she's pinched my baby."

Laura has helped Carmen to stand up, and is softly holding her palm against the trembling cheek. Susan stands looking into Carmen's eyes, as if offering to cry for her, if needed. "Well, you forced her to it," Laura says angrily. "You forget she is only a child."

"Pah!" Concha is rattling the baby against her shoulder as if to shake its tears back into its toes, like sediment. It works. The screams shake and settle lower and lower, until they curl only in the baby's curled toes. "She takes advantage of her size," says Concha. "She can work as well as any other twelve year old! And she is lucky not to be made a prostitute, like some of them. She is probably just what someone wants."

Laura looks at her in shock. She cannot stand the sight of her long, sensuous cheeks or her poufed hair. But there are no words to say to her.

"Pah!" Concha almost spits the word again. "I would have, given her security. She could have left the Martinez for good and stayed here. But now—get her out of here! Let her go back to the Martinez, let them send her back to the slums!"

Laura, stooped over like an old woman, her heart pounding, leads Carmen and Susan out the door, and calls for David to follow them. Carmen is trembling, but Laura catches a flicker of triumph on her face, which brings a small burst of hope to Laura's heart. Ah, Carmen, you *are* clever! Maybe you *will* survive somehow.

CHAPTER 20

Laura's Birthday

On the morning of Laura's birthday, Francisca comes into their room. Andrés has already said, "I was going to get you a . . . ,"as he does every year. Now Francisca has given Laura some nylons, so she will not look like a prostitute by walking barelegged in the street (Francisca agrees with Concha for once); and she has begun to serenade Laura with a birthday song—a love song to a "novia," a beloved sweetheart.

She sings the song with the same pursed mouth and kewpie eyes that Andrés makes whenever he is musical or playful. Laura cannot bear it. Never could. It was almost enough to save her from marrying him. If only he'd done it a little more often! Now, it is even more unnerving to see great, proud Francisca with those rolling kewpie eyes and stiffly rolling shoulders. Even worse, Francisca is really singing a love song. (Singing it to me!) This is terrifying. It makes Laura forget all recent closeness to Francisca, all the shared moments helping Carmen.

"My beautiful, my beautiful," sings Francisca, smiling confidently like a nightclub singer. Laura looks to Andrés for help, but he is automatically snapping his heels against the floor and moving his hips. Those same kewpie eyes! It's a family custom! Even Concha's little Miguel practices it, she remembers. All coy and stiffly seductive. (Davy, Susan, don't you ever!) How did they ever learn it? Who praised?

Francisca sings on, her shoulders hunching up—one, then the other—her eyes smiling coyly, happily. I cannot smile at kewpie eyes! And what if Francisca is really . . . if she means the song somehow?

"Thank you," Laura says uneasily, when the song is over.

"And Laura—remember, it is almost time for the celebrations, the big Independence parade. You will see all our celebrations, that will be for your birthday too!"

Then she is gone, shyly rushing out the door.

"Why couldn't you show more appreciation?" says Andrés. "She was so eager to please you for your birthday."

"Well—it made me feel strange."

Andrés laughs. "Because of the song? We always serenade people on their birthday! What the song is doesn't matter—any popular song is all right."

"Well—you never told me," she says, embarrassed. "Anyway, that's not it. That's not it. It's . . . that Francisca wants too much. It makes me uneasy."

Andrés laughs again. "We all want too much," he says. "We never get it, do we?"

CHAPTER 21

The Lost Children

A few days later Laura finds Francisca weeping silently in the hall. The sobs are giant ones, tearing at her gaunt, hunched-over body.

"Pobrecita," Laura says in awkward pity, Francisca slumps into her arms and cries as Susan would cry.

"Please. Come. Talk to me in my room," Francisca begs. She unlocks the door and leads Laura in. It is a monk's chamber, perhaps a hotel linen closet once. Just big enough for Francisca's bed and wardrobe; one hard chair, one window. The wall opposite the bed is completely covered with yellowed newspaper clippings, letters, tattered snapshots. The clippings are full of violence and strangeness. Stories of medical monstrosities and miraculous cures. Stories of La Violencia—-brutal murders, mass beheadings by bandit gangs in the provinces. At the center, a group of ads seeking lost children—those same ones Laura had asked Señor Vargas about. Always a faded, pale picture of the smiling child, as if it is already in another world. Sometimes there is a clipping beside it, telling of a found child, showing its smile beside an embracing parent. More often a murdered child, a run-over child. Sometimes Francisca has put the clippings together conjecturally, as if trying to solve the mysteries on her own. In the middle of the lost children, there is a picture of Francisca as a little girl. Laura recognizes it at once. The large almond eyes are shining, the strong mouth already sad; yet it lifts slightly, hesitant and hopeful.

"I was a lost child too," says Francisca, coming close behind Laura.

Laura jumps slightly, startled. "Do you mean that you were really lost?"

"I mean that nobody ever found me," says Francisca. "My mother could not stand me. She said I was too dark, she said I was a bad child. She still hates me—did you hear her shouting at me just now? Sometimes I think I am a mirror for her. She does not like to look in mirrors, but she knows it is bad luck to break one." She begins to weep again. Laura thinks maybe there is some truth in what she says. Of all the family, Francisca is the only one who looks like their mother, and her fierce, stern nature is most like Pilar's.

"I told you about Enrique," says Francisca, swallowing her tears. "He loved me. Or at least I thought he did. But nobody else did! And he lied to me." She pulls the straight hair back from her rough-textured face. "There were not many men who looked at me. The doctor in New York—I hated him!"

"Yes, he was terrible!" Laura remembers Francisca's compulsive douching and douching that weekend she visited them, and feels in her own body Francisca's revulsion for the doctor the maid service gave her to, revulsion for that whole miserable and cruel time.

"Now I am thirty-five," says Francisca softly, shyly. "No man has looked at me in years, and I cannot hope any more."

"But Francisca—there are other things besides marriage," says Laura. She does not add that marriage can be despair also, that it too can be a dead end, leaving you even more lost than before.

"*What* else is there?" Francisca challenges her. "Do you know how I make my living? I make lace and do needlework, which is picked up by a salesman each week for a few centavos. How much *he* makes from it, I don't know! Oh, I suppose I could go into smuggling, like Concha's husband, who is richer than he pretends to be—but how would I do that, Laura? How would I even begin? Or I could be a prostitute, except I am so ugly, and I would never feel clean again anyway. Tía Marta taught me needlework, and that's all I know. She would have taught me more, for she is the only one who loves me—but it's all *she* knows! What can an unmarried woman do, but make cobwebs for her coffin, make lace for a few centavos?

"But—you could go to school, couldn't you? Like Elena did?"

"Elena! Yes, she is the successful one! They never experimented on her, they never hated her! Oh yes, like Elena! And be a frozen face like Elena, never caring about anyone, hiding from everyone's sorrows, hiding from everything. Like Elena, yes!

"I am sorry, Francisca."

Francisca grabs Laura's arm and looks at her intently. "Are you really sorry? Then help me, Laura! Help me to go back there, get me back into the States. I cannot survive here!"

Fear pours into Laura. Terror. Why? Why am I so afraid? Francisca is my friend, she is becoming my sister, my real sister. So why am I afraid of her again? "Francisca," she says, trembling, "Francisca, I don't know what to do, I don't know how to help!"

"You have helped Carmen. Why don't you help me? What is the difference?"

"But I have been no use to Carmen at all—because of Concha she is back with the Martinez again, and I still don't know how to get her back from them!"

"You taught her things—you did something! For me, you do nothing. Why?"

Laura stares at the clippings on the wall. Loss. Death. Murder. Monstrosity. Faded little children's faces already lost when the camera was before them. Fading even then, gone now forever. Where is the love? Why has the automatic writing, her own trembling hand, her own madness, promised it again and again? Where on this wall, in this room, is the gift of love? The words are bitter in her mind, a slap, a false promise.

She wants to put her own baby pictures on the wall next to Francisca's. In her mind she goes home and tears them from her mother's album and brings them back. That winsome child in her blond curls, in a pale short dress, reaching up to touch a birthday cake that is set on a tall stool in a weedy yard. There, child, next to Francisca, next to the others.

CHAPTER 22

The Jewess

"My mother was like me," says Francisca. "Once I could have loved her. I did love her. She had a powerful soul. If she had lived in ancient times, the *Indios* would have made a myth about her. *I* would have made a myth about her.

"In Santa Marta, she was different from anyone else. They were going to cut down the trees in front of our house, and my mother—she screamed at them, 'Do not cut down these trees.' She went outside and put her arms around one tree, as if it were her lover. So they cut down that one last, and my father took her back into the house. She hated our house ever after. She looked out on the tree stumps. In a whisper, very angry she would say it again: 'Do not cut down these trees.' Finally, our father took us to Bogotá and we opened the hotel."

"I know," says Laura. "I remember Andrés told me that story many times. He loves trees too, you know. Whenever he sees a tree cut down, he remembers your mother."

"They called her the Jewess," says Francisca. "Because Papá was a moneylender and everyone hated him for it. They called us the Jews, but my mother most of all."

She is walking down the winding street of Santa Marta with two of her children holding to her skirts. She is carrying a basket of mangoes, cheese and bread, and they are going to the seashore to eat and swim. No one else ever does this.

Children of the town run after her, calling "The Jewess! The Jewess!" Their mothers do not stop them. After all, she has just been to collect money from some of them, with interest. They would call after her too, if they dared. Jewess! Wife of a moneylender!

"The Jews killed Christ!" the children shout.

Francisca looks around. Did her mother kill Christ? She tugs at the skirts. "Mother, did we kill Christ?"

"Stupid!" says Pilar. "We are not Jews! Don't we go to Mass on Sunday?" Francisca is reassured, but the screams of the children hurt her ears. She looks at Andrés, who is crying. Baby!

"Stop crying, baby," she whispers. "We are going to the seashore. We are the only ones who can go to the sea!" It is true. The sea is theirs alone, theirs and the Indian children's. None of the other townspeople go nearer than a stroll along the walk. It is improper to play in the sea! So Francisca and Andrés have this reward, at the end of the terrible walk. They play in the warm bay of Santa Marta, the soft, salt ocean. Their mother pulls up her skirts, smiles softly, and goes knee deep in the water with them. Oh Lord, how magnificent! Magnificent, the ocean! And it is ours.

"I wasn't lost then," says Francisca. "Not at the time, anyway. It must have happened later."

CHAPTER 23

The Origin of Hungry Souls

In the time long ago, there was a tree that reached from the earth all the way to the sky. The souls used to climb from branch to branch until they came to the lakes and rivers of the sky. There they would catch fish and also be blessed by the blossoms of the sky with much honey. One day the soul of an old woman could catch neither fish nor honey, and the other souls would not help her nor give her anything. In hunger and thirst, the old woman's soul became very angry, and she changed into a gnawing creature, which gnawed away at the tree until it fell. When the tree was burnt up, its sparks flew up to the rivers of the sky, but all the lamenting souls were left below. Some changed into parakeets and other birds and began short flights toward the sky, although they could not reach it. The condor and the hummingbird flew highest. Other souls despaired and were transformed into burrowing creatures, who dwelt in caves and under the earth, but their hunger followed them everywhere.

"It is sad that this had to happen," the gnawing creature said. "If only you had not been so unkind to me, when I was a woman and hungrier than you."

CHAPTER 24

A Small Glass of Fear

One morning Andrés and Laura are awakened by shouts and screams. It has been a bad night, with Susan crying out in a nightmare, frightening David so he couldn't go back to sleep. They are still groggy in their separated beds, and the children asleep at opposite ends of their bed, when Francisca rattles at their door angrily, and Andrés lets her in. She has hit Rosa, the young maid, who has been rushed to a doctor, bruised and frightened. Now Francisca grimly hands them their morning juice, a thick purple substance forced out of some strange fruit. She watches silently as they swallow the liquid. Laura nearly gags over hers, and when she finishes it Francisca begins to shout:

"It is your fault! Your baby cries in the night, you cough, make noise, and I cannot sleep. Then in the morning I am angry. I hit the lazy muchacha. Your fault!" She is speaking English, insistent and awkward. Laura likes her better in Spanish, when her words flow.

"We're sorry," Andrés tell her. "We didn't mean to keep you awake." He leads her to the only chair in the room, next to Laura's bed.

Francisca smiles at once; too suddenly, Laura thinks. "I know. I know you are sorry. I sorry too."

"That's good," smiles Andrés, squeezing her shoulder. With his thin, somber face and wavy hair, he looks much like the pictures of his father. He gives an extra tug now to the sash of the robe that was his father's, and takes his toothbrush, heading for the hotel bathroom, the one whose toilet seat was stolen by a guest.

Francisca moves over to sit on the edge of Laura's bed smiling broadly as she lights a cigarette. "I know what we do," she says. "You go with me today to the American Ambassador, you tell him to find my jewels and my suitcase, and I will have money to go back to the United States."

"But Francisca," Laura says. "We already did all we could to find your suitcase. They won't let me see the Ambassador. And the people who took your jewels sold everything long ago."

Francisca frowns and waves her cigarette under Laura's nose. "You are American, equal opportunity for all, the Ambassador will see you. If you like to help me, you help me."

"But I do want to help you." Laura notices that David is awake now, and frightened enough to be hiding under the covers. So it isn't just me!—Francisca *is* changing, she *is* frightening.

"Then if you want to help me, you *go*," Francisca shouts, and lapses into angry Spanish. Andrés returns, clean of mouth and fearless, and tries to reason with her, but she only grows angrier. "Traitors!" she shouts, walking out of the room like an avenging angel.

David is reaching around for his glasses, as if to examine the whole scene better. "They're on the floor, Davy!"

Susan jumps out of her bed and runs to Laura. "Why 'Cisca mad?" she asks, her voice a little uncertain, but plucky with two-year-old pride. "Pick me up. Mom!" Laura pulls Susan into her lap and begins brushing her dark blond curls. Davy has settled his glasses a bit crookedly on his nose. Such a dear little boy!

She turns to Andrés.

"Why *does* Francisca act this way?"

He has calmly continued dressing himself, and now sits down at the edge of the bed to begin his morning shoe ritual. "She has been like this before," he says, carefully smoothing out his stockings and folding them open in the special way he uses to pull them over his wide feet. "I never thought to tell you about it."

"Do you mean before the time she had the breakdown in New York and they had to put her on the plane?" Susan sits docile, comforted on Laura's lap, enjoying the brush strokes. But Laura is electric with unreasonable fear. The electricity goes into Susan's hair, makes it crackle and stand up.

"Once when she was very young," Andrés says, "She had to go for some months to the hospital and they gave her electric shock. She hated it. When she came back she was very calm, I remember. She was afraid *not* to be." He leans down to pick up his shoes. His left foot is propped on the right knee, and he slips the shoe slowly and carefully over the stockinged foot. Laura has always found it unbearable to watch this meticulous ritual, but whenever she complains of it he only laughs and boasts that his father always took twenty minutes to put his shoes on in the morning.

"Why didn't you tell me about Francisca?" Laura asks, as Susan jumps down from her lap. "How can you marry someone and not tell them there is mental illness in your family?" She is ashamed as soon as she says this. What she really means is, how can you marry someone without warning her how unhappy she is going to be, without warning her that you do not approve of ecstasy of any kind, that you will make her a lonelier stranger than she already was?

Andrés doesn't answer her shameful question until he has finished tying his shoes. Then he stands up and speaks to her with sudden bitterness. "You always have a label for things, don't you? You who are as strange and crazy as anyone! Don't speak that way about my family again. You have not even tried to understand them. You haven't even made an effort to get along with my mother!"

Laura leaps at the truth of this, if there is any. Anything to get away from the greater truths, the greater fears. "I'm sorry," she says. "I just can't seem to please her, so I don't try very hard any more. Andrés, yesterday she wouldn't even give me a towel for Susan's bath!"

Andrés looks at her kindly again, as if he too wants to leap away from the greater fears. But these shifts in feeling—how can we keep up with them? "I know," he says. "My mother is a bitter old woman. But she is brave. She has worked hard and now she is old—and still she must work. She is not easy to like, but—" He smiles charmingly. "Can't you pretend you're in the Peace Corps?"

"I'll try." Laura gives him painfully the smile he expects, as she finishes buttoning Susan's dress. Andrés lifts the child onto his shoulder, and beckons to his little boy, still in pajamas, but who has managed to get his shoes and a sweater on.

"Come, Susita, come on David—we will have breakfast together."

Laura watches them go. It is like Andrés not to wait for her, and one of the things she can't get used to. She shivers in the unheated room as she takes off the heavy pajamas they gave her because of the cold, and begins to dress. The fear begins to fade a little. How archaic of her, to talk about "mental illness in the family" as if it were a kind of curse. She *does* put labels on things. But Andrés puts labels on me too! "My wife" is one label. "Crazy" is the other one. He thinks the two are incompatible, but maybe it's the other way round! She smiles a little at that. But no, I was always a stranger.

Laura finds a pin to fasten her green plaid skirt, then stands before the mirror brushing her hair, studying her own sad eyes. Her hand trembles. If she dared to allow it, it could write messages, warnings maybe. She does not want to see the words. In that odd round scrawl so different from her own hand, words would appear. But from where? And why? She does not trust herself. She does not want to see the words.

CHAPTER 25

In Tía Marta's Room

In the evening after supper, the family gathers in Tía Marta's room, the only family place in the hotel, to tell her their stories and ask her mediation in their problems. All the little family dramas seek their light in Tía Marta's dilated pupils, in that dismal room. Is this the old woman's only life? Laura has heard Tía Marta mutter softly, begging God for release, and yet it is clear the family cannot do without her.

Laura feels out of place at these family gatherings and often stays upstairs, reading by a dim light, reading to the children until they fall asleep. But tonight she wants to show Andrés that she is trying. She has promised to join him there, after the children are asleep. Just as she softly closes the door of their room, Francisca stops her in the hall.

"Wait for me," she whispers. She lights a tall, fat religious candle, and they start down the dark circular staircase together. Against the curving wall, their shadows ripple along beside them, larger and stranger than themselves, ready to devour. Watching the shadows and listening to the shuffle of Francisca's slippered feet, Laura feels disembodied. She feels a secret oneness with Francisca, as if they know each other deeply. And yet she feels more frightened, more displaced than ever. In this country, Laura thinks, as she measures her steps to Francisca's, to really see is to feel great sorrow, great despair. And Francisca sees; she sorrows. I see too, but I am exile here. And it is not just this country.

There are things to see at home that I closed my eyes to. But here, now, what we share is deeper than country, more fearful and unknown. If there is anything we share.

The shadows nod, and Francisca smiles at her over the candle's distorting light. It is not a happy smile. Laura feels relieved when they reach the dim room where the others already sit, ghostlike, around Tía Marta's bed. Francisca rushes ahead without warning, announcing herself by singing the national anthem in her harsh voice.

It is clear the others have been discussing her, for they do not speak at once, and Elena begins a business of pouring *tinto,* the thick black coffee they drink after dinner. Francisca sings loudly to the end of the song, then stops. The early model television is showing Dr. Kildare in Spanish, flickering almost like a silent movie. Laura walks to Tía Marta's bed to greet her. She is as old as Pilar, but her face is still serene and beautiful, her eyes a clear, surprising blue.

"My leg is painful," Tía Marta tells her. "They did not send the girl with the heating pad and it has been hurting me all day."

Do you want to see a doctor?" Laura asks.

Tía Marta lets her head fall back on the pillow, into shadow. "No, the doctor is no use. But you are kind to ask." She leans forward again. "You are a good girl. You must try to understand us," she says, her voice sad and tender.

Andrés calls Laura to the table at the side of the room, where Elena has been pouring *tinto.* "Look! Elena has given us this Tairona sculpture for our anniversary! We have to keep it in Colombia because of the law—but it is ours!" He thrusts the heavy object into her hand. It is a time-battered pottery figure, leering at them with comic fierceness.

"How beautiful!" Laura turns to Elena with unexpected warmth.

Pleasure smiles through Elena's perfectly made-up face as she answers. "It is an authentic Tairona jaguar god. I am sorry you must keep it here—but maybe that will persuade you to stay longer." Laura is touched, for Elena usually remains so aloof. She is about to thank Elena when Francisca pounces forward and grabs the sculpture from her hands.

"Now, my brother!" she says to Andrés. "Now you take me to the Ambassador, or I will smash this!"

"Sí, Francisca," he says calmly. "I will take you. I will make an appointment tomorrow."

"We will see," she answers. "I'll take this to my room now, where it will be safe until I see the Ambassador. Come, my little friend from the Sierra, where jaguar gods devour what they want, and do not wait." She makes her free hand into a claw and paws at the air menacingly, hissing like a cat. "I am tired now. Goodnight! Be good or the jaguar will devour you." She laughs, then disappears from the doorway, the gift under her arm.

The family sits quietly, as if nothing has happened.

"How could you let her take it?" Laura asks Andrés. "She will drop it on the stairway, even if she doesn't break it on purpose."

"What else could I do?" he answers.

Tía Marta's voice rises like smoke from the bed. "When Francisca was a young girl, very pretty but a little too tall and growing too fast, and we were new to Bogotá, there was a doctor who offered to slow her growth with a new method. He gave her the hormones of men."

"You have said enough!"

"It was an experiment upon Francisca, but he did not tell us that," Tía Marta continues, her voice growing hard, as if the smoke were frozen to metal. "She grew even taller and her voice grew deep. Then hairs appeared on her face. She felt a great fear and cried every night."

"But she is a normal woman now," says Pilar. "She was not harmed."

"That is true," says Tía Marta. "But her spirit—her spirit was harmed."

"I did not know," says Pilar angrily. "I did my best. I trusted the doctor."

"You trusted Bogotá! You brought us to this cold place because of your cold dreams of money. Now we all suffer, and Francisca most of all."

"And if your brother had been a proper husband," says Pilar, "He would not have left all such things to me while he hid away with his books, and we would not struggle like this today. Haven't I cared for you? Don't you think 1 wish I could be in bed all day, like you, instead of working for hours on feet that ache?"

"And don't you think that I would like to be on my feet, even if they ached and I had to work hard, as you do?" Tía Marta's voice is soft again. "I know I am a burden. I know you do your best, hermanita. I am sorry."

"I am sorry too," says Pilar, her husky voice shaking. "We have said enough." She stands up from her place in the shadows and hobbles to the door, not stopping to say goodnight.

CHAPTER 26

The Gift

All the next day there is a *páramo,* the mist-like rain that hangs over the mountains and drifts down on the chilly city. Late in the afternoon it turns into a heavy rain, with water falling through the broken skylight into the patio garden. Laura runs through the falling drops on her way to their room. Suddenly she sees Francisca in the hall.

"Laura!" she calls. Laura stops by the door, as Francisca strides grimly toward her and hands her a newspaper clipping. "A gift," she says coldly, then walks away, not sister but avenging angel, fearful stranger.

"Gracias," Laura calls after her uncertainly. All the cold of the day rushes into her as she looks down at the clipping—a ghoulish drawing of a black-robed skeleton carrying a scythe and leering Death's leer. It's only a deranged woman's anger, she tells herself. But something inside seems to long for the fear, for extremes. It's a death threat, says an inner voice. A death threat from a madwoman, and you are in a foreign land, a foreign land. You will die. . . .

Laura runs to the kitchen to get Susan and David, who have been playing with Luisa, the cook. Without speaking to anyone she calls Andrés at his office in the National Archives, then locks herself and the children in their room, ignoring their protests. No more attempts to understand— she lets the ecstasy of panic sweep over her. At last, an ecstasy that is not forbidden! When Andrés arrives, she bursts into loud sobs, echoing all her childhood fears, all her fears in the marriage, her fear of Colombia. "I can't stay," she cries. "I'm afraid of her. You've got to send me home."

He pats her lightly on the back, the kind of comfort strangers give. "What can I do?" he says.

Elena comes in, tall and scornful, followed by their mother. They sit on the bed and look at her disapprovingly, as Andrés shows them the drawing. The children watch from their bed. Laura sees how frightened they are, and wishes she could take it back. And she sees how it hurts and bewilders Andrés, to be caught between her and his family.

"It was only a joke," says Pilar, glaring at her. "A joke."

Elena is silent at first. Laura knows she is repelled by her panic and embarrassed for Francisca. *Grosería* is the word she uses when disgusted by emotional outbursts. But she does not speak it now. Laura hears it anyway.

Andrés asks about Francisca's recent behavior. "Do you think she meant any harm? What about when she hit Rosa?"

"Hmmmp! That is nothing," says Pilar, her arms folded across her chest.

Laura feels ashamed. "No, she meant no harm," she says. "It is my own problem. When I leave, everything will be all right." *It is—oh, I see it now!—it is that I already brought my own picture of Death with me!*

Elena sighs. "You do not have to leave," she says. "This has been coming for a long time. Francisca must return to the hospital. We have no choice."

"Please don't! Andres, Please tell them the hospital is no answer. Tell them how she is afraid of shock therapy. Don't let them do it because of me!"

"It is not because of you," Elena breaks in coldly, pronouncing it carefully, in English.

The children are very quiet. They do not even know what questions to ask.

CHAPTER 27

But God Will Not Forgive You

It is the beginning of Independence week. The celebrations begin at 5:30 in the morning, when Laura is awakened by the sound of trumpets and the muffled noise of marching feet. Kneeling over Andrés's huddled, sleepy form, she opens the window, leans out to see the soldiers passing two blocks away, their bayonets glinting even in the dim morning light. She hears a voice call her name and looks down to see Francisca smile at her from the balcony below. Her smile shows nothing of yesterday's turmoil. Laura feels again a link between them, the two who watch the parade at dawn.

She looks at the children's bed where David is just waking up. "Come, Davy! It's a parade!" He bounces across the room, jumps over his grunting father, and snuggles beside her, peering out the window. "A parade!" he shouts. "Susie, a parade!"

It is an unusually warm day for Bogotá, with that rare sun that makes people run into the streets to catch its light. All day Francisca is calm. In the afternoon she works in the little patio garden, pinching off dead leaves and blossoms from the potted plants in olive oil and soda cracker cans and squat plaster models of Chipcha gods. The ends of her straight black hair fall against her cheeks as she bends lovingly over the plants. Susan, David and Miguel run back and forth excitedly, but Francisca does not play with them as she sometimes would; she suffers their noise, wincing slightly. Laura steals glances at her as she comes and goes throughout the afternoon. When their eyes meet Laura smiles shyly, Francisca reluctantly.

Francisca works with the plants all day, using a small rusted garden fork to turn the earth around them. When the warm sunlight has disappeared and the evening wind begins to blow through the broken panes of glass, Laura ventures into the patio once more on her way to dinner, puzzled to find Francisca still there. Susan is already with Luisa, practicing Spanish and begging for treats. Laura hesitates in front of Francisca now.

"Francisca—" She stops. Francisca's eyes catch at something behind Laura and her temples go suddenly white beside her dark eyes. She jumps to her feet, holding the little garden fork in front of her like a claw.

"Go away!" she shouts. "Don't touch me!"

Laura stumbles sideways, cutting her leg on the edge of a soda cracker can that holds a blooming fuchsia. She looks back to the door leading from the front hall, and sees Andrés standing behind a small dark man, neatly dressed, with a neat gray mustache. A larger form stands in the shadows behind them.

"Come, Francisca," says the man with the mustache. His voice is not unkind, not as cold as his appearance. "I am going to help you. We are old friends. Remember?"

"Leave me alone!" she shouts hoarsely. "Go away and leave me alone!" Andrés shrinks back through the doorway; the bigger man steps forward. Laura crushes the miniature orange tree as she backs into the corner, and tiny oranges roll past her feet. She tries to make her way to the dining room door, but Pilar appears on the threshold, standing with her arms folded.

The big man lunges forward, catching Francisca's wrist. The garden fork clatters to the tile floor as the smaller man moves quickly. A hypodermic needle flashes into Francisca's arm. Her scream tears into the air, into Laura's heart. Then, too abruptly it seems, she slumps into the big man's arms.

Laura stares over their heads at the two mountains blackening over the city. I made this happen! I did this! The statue of Christ on Guadelupe has been illuminated for the night, and on the twin peak of Monserrate, the lights are shining in Francisca's church of miracles. She dares not look at Andrés, or into the faces of any of them. Laura hears them lead Francisca out of the garden; she hears the echoes of the men's shoes and the ragged clatter of Francisca's sandals, stumbling down the stairway. Francisca was my only friend here, Francisca after all.

She turns to Pilar, words in Spanish forming on her lips before she wills them. "Forgive me," she says. I should have kept the fear away. It is fear that should be dragged down the stairs, its sandals clattering. Not Francisca.

Pilar looks at her coldly, her hard lips unyielding. "But God will not forgive you," she says. "Díos no le perdone."

Laura tries to answer, to explain. But she cannot speak. She needs Andrés, or someone. She looks down where Francisca's pink rubber garden gloves lie beside the rusted fork on the tiles of the patio. They look like discarded hands.

"I must get my children," she says.

It is the eve of Independence Day. Laura stays alone in the room with her children, reading stories to them, waiting for Andrés. The silence in the house is louder than the noises in the street. When Andrés comes in very late, he doesn't challenge her pretended sleep, and she does not try to share her guilt or fear. That is between her and Francisca, and they may never meet again.

There are firecrackers in the predawn hours, feeding the heart of the night with fire, and the drunks in the bar below sing louder and sweeter than ever before. In the morning there is a splendid parade, the one Francisca promised them, with soldiers in glittering Prussian helmets, and a mounted brass band playing from the backs of prancing horses. Laura tries to imagine the hospital, but only an empty cell comes into mind. She wonders if Francisca is awake, and if she hears the music too.

CHAPTER 28

Lamentation

In the days after Francisca is taken away, Concha's Siamese cat goes into heat. Can such a thing be coincidence? The cat moans and howls all about the hotel, day and night. Concha will not let it out to meet the unworthy cats below. It wails unbearably, wild female cries of imprisoned spirit. My heart's own cries.

Rain pours into the small patio where Francisca's hands still lie, where her scream still vibrates.

CHAPTER 29

The Cave of Nabulwe

At the foot of the Sierra Nevada de Santa Marta, a Kogi priest sits in meditation, communing with the Ancestors, seeking the wisdom of the Great Mother Nabulwe, who dwells in the snowy mountain. He twirls the stick in his gourd full of lime, and chews his coca leaves, which keep him alert always in his search for the divine. Life is devotion to truth; he blots out all other desires. He does not sleep. In the round huts with cone-shaped roofs, the women sleep alone with the children and are not allowed to chew coca leaves or share the men's rituals. Perhaps they do not need to. Perhaps they do. The anthropologists do not say; they do not even think to ask. Perhaps the Great Mother will not answer the men until they share their quest with women.

Francisca in her room in the hospital is not sleeping. Like the Kogi women, she has no coca leaves to chew, no little gourd and stick to trick her mind away from sorrow or desire. She has been taught no way to seek the Great Mother atop Sierra Nevada de Santa Marta, and the *Cristo* of Monserrate with his glass tear does not answer her salt weeping. The Virgin cannot be her goddess, for she is too demure and delicate, with her tiny hands and feet, to understand Francisca.

But I have heard of the mother goddess Nabulwe in the Sierra Nevada. Elena has told me of the *Indios* who live their lives in devotion to her, and I have read about them on my own. And I have known them in my dreams. Nabulwe is not too delicate for me; she has given birth to jaguar sons and jaguar daughters. I fly to her on my condor wings, and she welcomes me in her cave of ice. Here I lie down, and it does not matter if they assault my body with electric terrors, and it does not matter if they jab into my skin their ugly poisons. I am protected by the poison of the golden frogs. I become a child of Nabulwe and she gives me all the power of her children.

For now, I huddle in the cave of ice and wait until she tells me to go down the slopes, and find my own people, the ones who speak my secret language. . . .

CHAPTER 30

A Haunting

Andrés and Laura go for a walk in the evening. They walk to the Capitol and the Plaza de Bolívar, where the Liberator's statue stands illumined, small in the center of the great square. A few night pigeon sounds, occasional murmur of taffeta wing rustle.

Andrés is telling Laura about his economic studies of the urban social classes—technicalities of microfilm, of dust and discovery. Laura tries to listen, but she is wanting to talk about the bank that was bombed today, and could Señor Vargas be involved? Wasn't he acting strangely just before? She is wanting to talk about how Jacqueline Kennedy's new baby has been born and died, its name proclaimed in Bogotá headlines as if it had lived and accomplished. She is thinking of babies who never have names, whose dying goes unnoticed. What is named by the name of Patrick Bouvier Kennedy? Perhaps he whispered something, some message for the nameless ones. No, she cannot say these things to Andrés. And if she lets these thoughts go, others come—her fears about Francisca, her guilt and fear about herself. And always Pilar's voice echoing, "But God will not forgive you."

As they stroll across the square in the cold night mist, the square with its illuminated buildings around the edges, its lights shining darkly on the pavement, they see two small girls approaching them. The youngest is maybe five years old, and the oldest is nine or ten. She is carrying a baby in her arms, a heavy baby, almost old enough to walk. The five-year-old is holding onto her sister's ruana as they walk past rather swiftly, barefoot in the cold pavement. Their ruanas are thin and short, with rumpled cotton dresses hanging underneath.

Silently they pass, as if they have been haunting this square for a hundred years. The baby is heavy, but the older sister will never drop it, never let it fall to the pavement or float up to the sky. She can be depended on. Though they are ghosts, I see the brightness and the sorrow of their eyes. I see the sores on their small feet and the threads hanging from their torn hems.

Laura and Andrés turn away silently, walk back to the hotel almost in silence. When they reach the little bars on their street, she begs once more to go in with him and listen for a time to the warm, comforting guitar songs. He is annoyed that she should ask again.

"You know women are not allowed in the bars."

"Even tourists?" she asks.

"But you are not a tourist—you are my wife," he says.

"Then I will stand here and listen on the sidewalk." She stops, cementing her feet to the pavement, almost weeping. Song and golden light flow from the swinging doors, while in the window the shadow figure of a story-teller lifts his arm in enchanting gesture. What story is he telling? Whose story? He makes her think of Francisca and her love of stories. Who does she tell them to now, to herself alone?

Andrés gives her a few minutes, almost counting them, then firmly takes her arm. "We have to go in now," he says. Laura uproots her feet and walks slowly across the street with him.

Hilario, the grim young porter, responds slowly to their banging on the door. He lets them in with a scowl. "Buenas Noches," says Andrés as they pass him, but he doesn't answer. "I don't like him," Andrés mutters, loud enough to let him hear.

"No one does," says Laura, when they are halfway up the stairs. "Why did your mother hire him?" (Because his scowl is just like hers?)

"She says the fellow needed a job. Because he is from the provinces and did not get working papers here, it is illegal to hire him. La Violencia . . ."

"But isn't that stupid, to judge a person by where he is from?"

"Maybe. My mother thinks so anyway. She hates bureaucrats, so she gave him this chance—but he doesn't seem too grateful for it! I think he is the one stealing money from her office. I told her that yesterday, but she won't listen."

They are at their door. Andrés pulls the key from his pocket, still talking, as if he has been waiting for a chance to bring this up. "I also think he may be influencing Concha's older son. Pablo is spending too much time with him—maybe I will take him away with me soon—for a little journey. Get him away from here."

"Not without me," says Laura, her voice beginning a command, but ending with a questioning note; a question with a touch of warning in it. "Not without me?" Not with Francisca gone! Not with all I am afraid of here!

"Let's wait and see," he says, pushing the door open. Sweet, round-faced Rosa has been watching the children; they send her away with a little money. Laura bends over her sleeping children, thinking of Patrick Bouvier Kennedy and his small, private death. Thinking of those girls walking like ghosts across the square. Light from the street comes through the louvered blinds as she sits down on the children's bed, one hand resting on Susan's gently moving back, the other on David's sweet head. Music rises from the bar down below and mingles in Laura's mind with the children's old bedtime songs. Sleep my child and peace attend thee . . . I know an old lady who swallowed a fly . . . perhaps she'll die! (Davy and Susan giggling in their beds at home.) I hardly sing for them at all here, I never sing, we don't play any more. Laura longs to wake them up, sing and tickle: I know an old lady who swallowed a spider . . . it wiggled and jiggled and *tickled* inside her!

Andrés comes back from the bathroom and climbs into his bed. Laura's Mama Bear bed awaits her. But this bed is too hard. The great wardrobes separating their beds are like fat old soothsayers, muttering "no more love, no more love."

A few blocks away, three children are gliding like ghosts across the Plaza de Bolívar. The Liberator, standing in the center, watches them sadly. The baby falls from the oldest one's arms and goes floating toward the star that shines through the night mist. The other two children jump on tiptoes, arms stretched up to catch it. A wind picks them up, and they follow the baby through the sky. The Liberator slowly cranes his neck. Ah. There they go.

CHAPTER 31

The Condor Woman

Once there was a woman who was the daughter of a giant, set down among small people. She was a daughter, indeed, of the jaguar goddess. She herself was not a jaguar, though sometimes she took on jaguar ways and devoured victims in the moonlight. This was not the way of her heart, however. She wandered lonely by day and by night, for she belonged nowhere. She felt the sufferings of the people and animals of the forest, and she knew not what to do. Sometimes she would go into a frenzy of sorrow, which frightened others. Finally she was betrayed. She was bound up and taken away to a hut outside the village where an evil shaman tortured her.

During her torments, the woman's heart leaped out of her and into the sky. Her heart stood at the top of a rainbow and looked down on the world. Oh world I know you! it said. When her heart flew back to her, it brought with it the form of a great, powerful and far-seeing bird, and the woman was changed into a condor. Then she could fly into the highest mountains and join the proud ancestors who had retreated there hundreds of years before, refusing subjugation. Although the condor was a bird of prey, she was a noble bird, sparing many captives and seeing far. She had great devotion to the mother goddess and to the secret wisdom of the universe, and used to fly to the highest peaks, there to contemplate truth.

CHAPTER 32

Journey

Andrés wants to take a trip to the coast with his nephew Pablo. "He needs a father figure," says Andrés. "You can stay here. It will be too much for you to come along."

Laura looks at him in amazement, terror. "You would leave me here? After all that has happened?"

"You will be all right," he says. "Francisca is in the hospital now. There is nothing to frighten you."

"Andrés, don't you understand anything? Don't you know it is even worse because Francisca is in the hospital? Your mother and sisters hate me now. I hate myself now!"

"Why?" He comes out of his preoccupation to look at her seriously a moment. "It wasn't your fault, you know. Francisca was sick before. Why should you blame yourself?"

Francisca was my only friend here, my only friend. How can she tell him? There are subtleties of betrayal too fine, too sad for words. All she can do is insist that he take her with him.

The long, lurching train ride makes her feel that things will change. They make their descent from the Andes, through the *páramo*, the hanging, misty rain. Past the mountain shrine where Christ sits encased in glass, as if waiting in an eternal phone booth. By accident, someone will dial a wrong number and love will answer.

Laura looks constantly from her window, as if in a dream. In a deep chasm cut by a river, she sees a cave in the stone wall; the naked spider form of a baby sleeping there, like a small sacrifice. Perhaps it will sleep there forever, until the river rises and takes it from the cave, accepts it, receives it. Appeased, the river god will lend its waters to the sky, the land will be nourished, there will be food for the many. But now the baby lies there, naked, unknowing, unseen—for the train has already rushed by—has it been sacrificed already? Is it dead or only sleeping? Which god will take it now, which god takes the children?

In the night the train stops. Laura jerks awake and looks out the open window to see fireflies in the dark. Men's voices, brief shouts and cries. Can it be bandits? Will La Violencia reach us after all? You will die in Colombia . . . perhaps it will be now.

But she does not feel any fear. The night is strange. It is strange to have this open train window with night air blowing in, fireflies flickering like eyes in the dark, or stars come very near. She looks at Andrés beside her, his head fallen back in sleep. Across the aisle his nephew Pablo sleeps, one arm dangling. Susan and David are jumbled together, stretched out on the seat opposite them, David's sleeping face in a worried little scowl like his father's, Susan's fists curled like a baby's, like white flowers glowing dimly in the darkness.

Things will change on this journey. We are of good will. We love our children. We will learn to love each other after all.

Not understanding his country has made him seem farther from her. I do not love your country, she whispers in her heart. I do not love your country, it is cruel and violent, though it is beautiful and breaks my heart. And your warrior mouth that so fascinated me once, I wish it were a poet's mouth instead, or a lover's mouth. She imagines in the dark that she can see the strange, harsh lines of his lips. She knows by memory how when he wakes his eyes will be innocent and dark, opposite to that mouth. Once I called him my flower-in-the-morning husband because of his eyes when he first awoke, nearsighted and undefended, sweet. But they never gave what they promised, somehow. Moments of sweetness in the morning, yes. But then the fear of woman would arise in him, the taboo against a woman's need, and her desire would be denied sharply, insistently, at the most painful moment. Oh! And in the day, his eyes would look far, far ahead, through those rose-tinted lenses he wore.

The train lurches forward, as if the pain of her memories had lain on the tracks and been heaved suddenly away. She leans back, letting her eyes rest on the white roses of Susan's sleeping hands. Letting the petals of her eyelids fall.

CHAPTER 33

Santa Marta

In the morning she wakes to see a torch-bright flowering tree, like a flag at the foot of the mountains. Heavy warmth. Sudden closeness of palm forest, banana forest outside her open window, and cicadas roaring louder than the train. Why can't our marriage be a journey like this, from the cold regions to the warm?

As the train stops, boys selling ices run to the windows, reaching the brightly colored ice batons to the outstretched hands of the thirstiest passengers. Concha's Pablo has his centavos ready and is one of the first to retrieve a glowing, magenta treat. Andrés hands him one of their suitcases and takes the other two himself. Tense with joy and anxiety, he leads them to the town he was born in, holding David's eager, upstretched hand. Laura, holding Susan, stumbles after them, down the iron steps of the train, into the winding streets of Santa Marta. The boys with their ices crowd after them until they buy bright yellow ones for the children—pineapple!—and magenta for themselves.

"The streets wind like this because of pirates," says Andrés. "If invaders came ashore they would not know where to run. They would get confused, and the defenders could overpower them." He swallows the last of his ice with a slight slurping noise, charming to Laura.

"Did it work?" She is still nibbling at hers, gazing around them at the quaint and painterly curve of the street, the tile roofs, the occasional shy palms.

"Sometimes." He smiles. "Let's see if it works on you."

"I hope I'm not an invader," she smiles in return. "But I'm already confused." She hugs one sticky child and pats the head of the other. Her heart opens to Andrés. This is his birthplace. You are here, she thinks. I will find you here. I will learn to love you here.

CHAPTER 34

The Maracaibo Baseball Team

The Maracaibo Baseball Team is a roistering pageant of Latin virility. The sedate little beachfront hotel trembled at their arrival, but Laura enjoys the change they have brought. Proper Colombians from the interior, who make Santa Marta their ultimate shore, and cool Europeans who come here for quiet, make her feel Bogotá's coldness all over again, in the midst of this coastal heat.

But there is no coldness in the Maracaibo Baseball Team. Andrés has hated them from the moment they stole his bathing trunks from the balcony, or perhaps from before. Laura is secretly amused by this, for he stares at them in anger whenever they pass in the lobby, and on the beach he watches them closely, trying to locate his bathing trunks, which the thief among them (if they are not all thieves) is too clever to wear.

Laura watches them too, from the perspective of sand castles Andrés makes for the children. She looks past his softly sandy turrets to their shore choreography, sees them tumbling from one another's shoulders, tossing one another into the sea. Loud and laughing, small beyond her husband's towers.

Andrés has a talent for sand castles. Intricate and noble architectures rise under his hands, while Pablo, with his lazy, half-closed eyes, watches in silent adolescent mockery,

while Davy and Susan joyously help dig. As for Laura—
Andrés has done little lately that she can love as much as
these creations (nothing since that delicate slurping of magenta ice), and so she heaps much stored-up admiration on
them. For she is a woman who needs to admire before she
can love. "How beautiful they are! Like story book castles,"
she says. He laughs proudly, boy-like, building on. And she
lies in the sun watching turrets grow higher, while knightly
little figures gleam in the distance.

Close up, in the hotel dining room, the Maracaibo Baseball Team is a bouncing conglomerate of dark, smiling faces
and lively eyes. They are crude, noisy, frightening—but the
name "Maracaibo" embroidered extravagantly on their silk
shirts recovers for Laura something lost, as the sand castles
do for Andrés. She remembers the name from years ago
in school, when Lake Maracaibo was a blue shape in Venezuela, connected by a narrow channel with the sea, and
she heard a ring of adventure whenever she pronounced its
name. Maracaibo. In curling satin letters, arabesques. Now
here are its heroes, resting up before demolishing (for she
is sure they will) the baseball teams of Cali and Popayan,
drab interior places with no blue lake connected to the sea.

That lost ring of adventure, was that what confused her
into marrying Andrés? How could I have known that behind the ardent voice telling of revolution would be another voice echoing old denials and repressions? Behind those
Spanish phrases of seduction, the old rhetoric of guilt? Or
did I know somehow? Did I choose these boundaries after
all, when I thought I was helplessly chosen? Muñeca de
ropa, muñeca de palo, muñeca de plata—enchanting little seduction chant for midnight in Chicago's subway. Rag
doll, stick doll, silver doll. A doll is a doll in any language.
Not a woman. Didn't I know?

Now he has brought her to Colombia and his mother's
narrow beds. She hoped on this coastal trip to find some
new closeness with him, some warmth, some meaning that

would release her from her guilt about Francisca. But at the hotel she sleeps in one room with Susan, where a great propeller on the ceiling works fitfully to stir the air; and Andrés shares another room with Pablo. They are never alone together, and she is sure he wants it that way. It's true, he shared his homecoming eagerly. He showed her a walled garden, saying, "That is where I went to school," and then a pale yellow house-front with barred windows on the main square, saying, "That is where I was born. That was our house. There are the stumps of the trees my mother fought for." And she remembered in imagination her stern old mother-in-law in younger form, shouting in vain to protect those phantom palms and having her heart broken one more time. It is Andrés's favorite story about his mother, the refuge of his love for her.

But the house is now part of the police station, the tree stumps are desolate, and the heat deadening. When Andrés and Laura walked through the heavy night to visit old friends of his family, they found the people under bright bare light bulbs, sipping Coke and slowly waving woven fans. "They haven't moved in a dozen years," he told her later. They were delighted to see him, yet his return made no change in the rhythm of their fans.

The beach front is a relief from the thickness of the town air. At night the young people promenade up and down the walk overlooking the beach, and stop at outdoor cafes for drinks or ices. They are so young, Laura thinks. They can feel love even here in the heat and the dead town. They can find the edge of the ocean inside them and embrace on its beach. I have given away my youth, the part that is past and the part still unfolding. But to whom? Andrés does not receive it, perhaps I do not really give it. If I find my own shore, I am alone there.

On their third day at the beach, Andrés abandons her and the children. "Pablo and I are going inland to his father's village," he says. Does he really care so much for this sulky nephew? "I want you three to wait for us here. It will be only a few days." All right. Some need of his own he is following too. She argued enough not to be left behind in Bogotá. At least she has come this far, found this shore.

The Maracaibo Baseball Team glance at her more, now that Laura and her children sit in the tiled dining room alone. She has forgotten that people used to tell her she was pretty, before she married. She feels pleased and frightened to discover that again, takes more care with how she looks. But never looks into their eyes. Facing straight ahead, she holds Susan's reaching-up hand as Davy runs in front of them, into the dining room, or out onto the beach, where the waves splash at their ankles and the children laugh.

Still, she likes the feeling of those unknown male glances, warming through her skin. At dinner she puts all her gaze on the children's *cafe con leche*, the only milk the hotel will serve, and no help for getting a child to sleep. She urges them a dozen times to drink it quickly, glad they drink it slowly. For what else is there to do, after all? Go to their room, sit on the ugly iron bed, and translate dog-eared Spanish comic books until first Susan and then David falls asleep.

One evening after dinner she finds a key has been slipped under her door. Lifts it up, reads the number on the wooden paddle, and knows it is an invitation. How wonderful, she laughs. The Maracaibo Baseball Team has chosen me! Desires me! Or—wants to laugh at me? She feels nervous, frightened and excited. What if they are really laughing at her, clumsy gringa goodwife? And why is it so impersonal, with only this key? And yet that appeals to her in a strange, abstract way. Haven't individual men always disappointed? Andrés most of all, promising adventure, then putting her on a shelf. But the Maracaibo Baseball Team—! She has barely met the eye of one of them, yet she is conscious of them all—their eyes on her like one man's eyes, without one man's possessiveness. And so they have seen through her.

In the middle of the night, in the dark, she puts the key in their door and softly it opens. There is dim, rosy-yellow light from Aladdin lamps. One shadow figure lifts his arm in enchanting gesture. What story does he tell? Is it her story? Like Arabian Nights princes, princely dancers in silken loincloths rainbow-colored, her lovers glide forward to greet her, all smiling the same misty smile. While the storyteller—her real lover! (Wasn't it he who waited for her in that glowing bar in Bogotá when Andrés would not let her in?)—silently continues his enchanted tale. From dancer to dancer she moves, like Rita Hayworth in late-night movies with the sound turned low. In heavy silence, as under water, the movements slow, she glides from one to another until softly they become one. She knows them all in one low-volume swoon.

But this dream is too gentle! This is not the Maracaibo Baseball Team. The silken rainbow loincloths are sweaty jockey shorts. The enchanting gesture is a pitcher winding up, spitting on his hands. The silence is laughter. Silver doll, stick doll, rag doll. I am afraid. (Don't laugh at me!)

"Look," Laura says, smiling at David. "Look, here is an old key we don't need. You can throw it over the balcony and watch it fall." His sturdy small hand grabs the wooden paddle happily. Laura leads the children to the balcony; they laugh together as the key falls, the little wooden paddle making a maraca clatter on the pavement.

"Let's go get it. Mommy. My turn!" cries Susan. Do it again!"

"We have another key," says David helpfully. He runs to the table by the door, and brings her their room key. "Susie can do it too!" But no, she tells them, we have to go to bed now. Have to read a story first.

Oh yes, she thinks, when they are asleep at last—maracas in the silence, not laughter. And they will compel my eyes with theirs. (The blue lake and the loss.)

But Andrés did that—compelled her eyes with his, chanted his seduction chants. It came to nothing; it only trapped her in his vision, his narrow world. Like Rima caught in the pupils of her lover's eyes, he who never learned her language. Is entrapment all that ever comes of it? And is it really entrapment, if she has two such wondrous children? Oh, she longs to know, wishes she could understand.

And yet, and so, she turns away from that Maracaibo smile, from bare, outer essence of the mystery, hard muscles and sure bodies, because she fears no angel waits within them. No freeing angel in them or in herself. How could there be? (And don't they sing too, behind those cafe doors, and keep *their* women out?)

Wakeful in the middle of the night, she imagines the noise of Andrés's return in the room next door. But it is too soon for him to come. No, it is too late. It is a matter of indifference. So much, at least, they have taught her. Laughing and frightened, to the tune of the faltering ceiling fan, she makes a song to her lovers and lulls herself to sleep again—not caring that they will not hear her, not caring whether she means it or not, for they are her dream lovers now, and even she can laugh at that.

> Oh Maracaibo Baseball Team
> I am your lake
> with narrow passage to the sea;
> come swim in me!
>
> Oh Maracaibo Baseball Team
> I am your diamond;
> come swing in me!
>
> Oh Maracaibo Baseball Team
> come give me back
> your key!

CHAPTER 35

The Girl Mad about Honey

This story was first told in the time long ago. It has many endings depending on whether the story teller is a man or a woman, and on how much yearning and how much honey are in the world whenever it is told. The ending you will hear this time is neither the saddest nor the happiest of its many endings, but this is how it was in one time long ago:

There was a young girl of the gringa tribe, who was mad about honey. But she did not know what honey was, or where to find it. She wandered through the forests seeking honey, but never finding it. One day a woodpecker told her that he knew the secret of honey and that he would reveal it to her if she married him. And though she was doubtful, she agreed to marry him, for he was a scholarly woodpecker who read many books. But the woodpecker did not give her any honey.

He took her away to a new forest, where she met many strange creatures—jaguars, frogs, hummingbirds and condors. But all were as hungry as she was, and none knew the secret of honey. She was frightened in the new forest and cried out at night.

Meanwhile the woodpecker went about his business, hiding his secret store of honey in the trees. He was afraid that if he gave it to his wife, she would devour him along with the honey. To add to his fears, the bees had told him there would soon be a great drought, when everything in the forest would dry up. The honey would all turn to amber, and small creatures would be encased in it forever, until millions of years later, when archaeologists might dig them up and study them. This made the woodpecker very nervous. Since he was a scholarly woodpecker, he felt that if anything was to be preserved in that way it must be his books. And so he set about stealing all the honey in the forest before it could harden, and encasing his books in it. Then he made everything very small and stored it in the trees. And that is the origin of microfilm.

Meanwhile the girl mad about honey, abandoned by the woodpecker, wandered disconsolate in the dry forest. There one day she met a hummingbird.

"You are the only one I have not asked," she said. "Do you know the secret of honey?"

"I do," said the hummingbird. "The secret of honey is that first you must know the secret of flight." And so it taught her that, and she flew away into a different world, where the flowers always had dew on their petals and nectar within.

But the girl mad about honey found that she was so weary she could no longer taste the nectar. Sadly she flew into a great tree, where she changed into a golden tree frog and dwelt in the small pool of a hollow in the tree. There she drank rain water and ate the small flies, and waited to see if that would be all.

CHAPTER 36

Cartagena

Cartagena, the walled city. Andrés, in a guilty burst of attentiveness, has brought Laura here with Susan. Pablo has stayed behind in his father's village, so they are a simple family again. Throughout the rugged bus ride from Santa Marta (wild driver, egged on by pictures of the Holy Family, the Saints and Martyrs above his windshield), the long wait at the ferry at Barranquilla, and the final journey to Cartagena, Andrés was full of tenderness and charm. It is, Laura knows, the way he always turns to her when she loves him least. But here in Cartagena, the most beautiful of cities, she does not want to think about it. Perhaps they both know it is too late, or nearly so. Yet they are here. Cartagena.

This simple, lovely Hotel Miramar next to the sea. For the first time in Colombia they share one bed. Because of an electricity shortage, the lights are turned out in half the city. So they have eaten by candlelight in their small, clean room. When the candle is blown out, in sound of the sea, at last they turn to one another. Laura cannot help it. Hope rises in her, though a voice inside is saying, "You know better, you know." She cannot help it, she is happy just now.

In the morning they wake to the sound of canaries and of the ocean. The waves are visible from their open window. Gray and silver, dreamlike waves. The hotel is all white and blue. White stucco, naive madonna-blue woodwork. In the stone-latticed dining room where ivy grows along the wall, caged canaries sing contentedly. A breeze. Porridge.

CHAPTER 37

Into the Conch Shell

For a whole day, happiness. They take a launch across the long, placid bay to Bocachica, the narrow entrance to the bay, where castles stand guard on either side, just as they did when Cartagena fought off pirates. A friendly young priest in white robe chats with Andrés. Three happy, girlish nuns of St. Vincent de Paul, with their medieval swan-like headdress, play light-heartedly with Susan.

"Look at that ruin," says Andrés. "It was a leper colony once. They neglected the lepers so badly that finally it had to be evacuated. Then it was bombed by warships to keep anyone from settling there and catching the disease." A low, ancient-looking ruin on a wild stretch of shore. In the Flaubert story, St. Julien embraced the leper, who then revealed himself as Christ. And here—people so homeless they would move in after lepers, if a bomb did not prevent them. But there has been no embrace, no miracle, no revelation. Only the silence remains, the ancient leper mystery, as the launch glides past.

From the dock at Bocachica they rent a heavy, rough-hewn dugout canoe from young black boys, descendants of the slaves who were brought here centuries ago. The boys, friendly and spirited, paddle them around the castle to the fishing village with its thatched-roof huts. Andrés takes Laura and Susan to a small eating place the priest told him about, where a thatched roof extends over the open dining area and piglets root under rough board tables. A gentle woman with a clinging baby balanced on her hip serves them rice and a delicate-tasting fish called *urel*.

From the doorway, a handsome one-legged man, another descendant of the slaves, watches ironically. Whatever he knows, it clearly is a powerful knowing, includes extremes of ocean and danger. He has come back from that to stand in this rough doorway, watching tourists experience his shelter as if *it* were an extreme, an edge. His knowledge and irony are all he has over them, but that is something like enough.

In the afternoon they return by dugout to the fortress, gliding so close to the walls of the castle that they can see the fine grains of the stone, and the moss that grows on it. The canoe is so solid it barely lists, as Andrés holds Susan near the edge, letting her lean out to trail her hand in the water.

Through the main gate of the castle and across its courtyard; then across a stone bridge over the saltwater moat where Spanish ships used to hide in ambush. Suddenly they are at a tourist beach—a great shallow bath of warm water, too tame for swimmers, yet crowded with people happy to sit in a giant bathtub together. Susan plops down at once, waist deep and splashing with joy.

"Come, David," says Andrés to his son, "Let's make another sand castle. Just like the real castle over there!" Just what David loves most, and before long Susan has joined them too, almost spoiling some of her brother's best towers. Laura stays with them long enough to shape a clumsy turret and crenellate it with her index finger, but in a little while she wanders off, thinking of Santa Marta and Maracaibo, of Francisca, of her own heart's mysteries. Shells are everywhere. She begins examining them, washing them in the lapping water or holding them to the light. Some she keeps, and though she has some inner way of knowing which ones to bring, leaving many behind—still her handbag grows heavy with wet, sandy treasure: philosophical bits of brain coral, worn-away nautilus shells with the sea showing through their spirals, a serene moon shell.

One of the village boys runs up to sell her a great pink conch for only two pesos. He grins at her joy. Already to Laura it is a lifelong treasure, with its wide, rosy opening like a piece of sunset, and its secret windings, echoed outside by the spiky spiral crown, resembling a temple tower of Angkor Wat. She thinks ahead to times unknown, when this shell will rest on a mantel or a window sill, looking out on snowy fields perhaps, or maples in summer, Mediterranean pines, or a black desert night. What life will she be living then? She senses that it will not be anything she can predict now. She will not be this same Laura. Not the me I am now, half in one world and half in another, clouded in dreams, but without a vision.

The conch glows when she holds it up to the sun, as if it may hold the vision, have her life and its meaning reeled up inside it like a movie film. Her present is there too, a humming inner life that goes on implacably, and that she senses will survive as many years or as many lives as she chooses to put it through, no matter how absently, how inadequately she may live. It does not seem to press her too hard just now, to live more knowingly, to be wiser or stronger than she is. And yet it spins on, and she feels overwhelmed by its beauty—the beauty of her own life, of any life held up like the conch, to the sun. Perhaps those words that her hand wrote, that made her so afraid of madness, came from this hum inside the conch. The gifts of love, the threat of death. Words confuse the message. She lets them go back to the hum, to the spinning conch.

"Look." She shows the conch to Andrés and the children. Places it in the courtyard of their castle, like a spaceship from Venus, just landed. They smile, accepting it. And the castle's inhabitants are not terrified, for they have dreamed of this visitation for years, and the terror has at last been washed away. With elation, they approach the conch in their courtyard and enter it, ready for interstellar voyage.

Childhood dreams of shooting through space come back to Laura. How terrified I was then! I used to pray not to dream, but the dreams would come anyway. Shooting past all the stars and planets that were family, neighbors, teachers—past all of them into empty, starless space. Suddenly the childhood dream is wonderful, a blessing. Laura, too, walks from her sandy tower room, down the circular staircase, into the courtyard, into the broad opening of the rosy shell with its spiral crown like a temple of Angkor Wat. Is her family with her? All is so silent she cannot tell.

"Look!" cries Susan. Laura lifts her eyes from the conch to see a dugout canoe coming in to the beach. The three nuns in their swan-like headdress have transformed it into a delicate sailboat. Two young villagers leap out of the dugout to draw it onto the beach. Their dark bodies wet and gleaming, they offer their hands to the nuns, who step onto the sand like graceful white birds after flight, coming to rest.

CHAPTER 38

My Papá's Touch

I am riding, swaying, with Laura and the little ones in the horse-drawn carriage, driving along the shore back to the hotel, my eyes on the horse's straw hat with his ears poking through—when it happens again. A touch. A tap on my shoulder. A voice in my mind—Papá's voice, saying "Andrés. Andrés. Come."

The first time was in Chicago, the day Papá died. I was walking through the deserted university, under the gargoyles, one night during Christmas vacation. Everyone had gone home except the foreign students, and I was feeling very lonely, when it came. That touch on my shoulder, that soft call in his voice. "Andrés!" For a moment I felt he was walking beside me, his feet moving in the same rhythm as mine, echoing slightly on the pavement. I never guessed what it meant until a week later, when the letter came from Elena. The funeral all over by the time they let me know! Still, he spoke to me. He found me.

The second time was this morning, in the castle of San Felipe de Barajas. I was holding Susita, and Laura was walking beside me through the thrilling dark tunnels the Spanish made. The guide was showing us all the details of diabolic, labyrinthian design, and I was engrossed in admiration: the sudden turns, where soldiers running in the dark would break their heads if they did not know the pattern. The ingenious acoustics of the Spaniards, designed so whispers could be heard the length of a tunnel, so that messages, warnings of danger, could be spoken through the acoustic tube of stone connected to the city wall, and voices be heard from shore to castle, from castle to shore. The steep descending tunnel that forced us to walk faster, where Susita began to cry. Then the guide turned out the light to show us the complete blackness. *Such* blackness! Like before the Creation, before there was light. And then it happened, the touch on my shoulder. The whispered "Andrés!" from another shore. I wanted to tell Laura, but couldn't—for wouldn't it encourage her own mysticism, which I am sure is dangerous, outside the blessing of the Church? But this—this is different, for it comes from my own Papá. For that reason too, I could not speak of it; it is so private, this touch, it brings tears to my heart. This morning, in San Felipe's castle, I thought it was only a memory of the time in Chicago, a mystery brought on by the blackness of the labyrinth.

But here—now—riding at dusk in this carriage, with the sound of the horse's hooves in front of us, with the warm sea wind, with blue waves just there at our left, I am afraid it is not a memory. The touch lingers, just as when a living person touches you. I am afraid something is wrong at home; I will have to call home at once. I will have to tell Laura.

CHAPTER 39

Her Dreaming Blood

"I found her here." Calm, dry of voice, Elena shows them the spot on the floor of the lofty bedroom, on the other side of the plywood hotel partition, where Pilar bled to death from the slit in her throat. From above the wooden wardrobe, the great portrait of Pope Pius XII continues to look down at the stain. Apparently the Holy Father never moved, never expressed alarm, not even in the instant when Hilario threw her down, grabbed the two hundred pesos from her opened safe, and ran.

There the Pope remains, his hand raised in mild blessing, blessing victim and murderer alike. My children. From the other wall the young Pilar continues to look down serenely, lily in hand, still dreaming of her first love, not yet having lost him to his broken breaths, not yet having married Francisco or lost him, not yet having borne children or sorrows. Did this gentle young Pilar leap into the old Pilar's body before she died, so that all the Pilars might rise together? Did some of her dreaming blood run out with the rest?

CHAPTER 40

Francisca

"We must get Francisca," says Andrés. "She cannot miss the funeral as I missed Papá's."

Elena smiles sadly, remembering. Without any makeup, she is very pale, undefended. "She is already home. I went to get her yesterday." Two sisters riding home from the mental hospital in a taxi. One tells the other about a terrible madness that has taken place. One comforts another.

"Is she all right?" Andrés asks. Laura listens anxiously. *Is* she all right?

"She is very strong," says Elena. "Maybe stronger than any of us. Concha is frightened for her children and has gone with them and her husband to a friend's house. I am . . . as in a dream. But right now, Francisca is with Tía Marta, giving comfort."

Andrés, who has hardly been able to speak since he had the news, who got them swiftly back to Bogotá but in terrible, agonized silence, seems to shed some of his pain as he hears this. "Let's go see them."

Francisca is sitting next to Tía Marta's bed, holding the older woman's hand; neither of them is speaking. Silver lines shine on Tía Marta's worn face, but she is calm. Francisca is thinner, her eyes softer, as she stands to meet them. Andrés walks forward, embraces his sister, and then sits down on Tía Marta's bed to kiss her cheek, hold her two hands in his.

Laura stands back, not wanting to intrude. Hesitantly, she sits on a straight chair near the door. Francisca comes to her, taking a seat on the old stuffed chair in the corner, turning toward Laura, measuring her almost. With searching looks, each finds the changes in the other.

"It is all right," Francisca says.

Still, Laura must say it. Pilar's words still echo. "I am very sorry—for everything."

"I know."

"Can you forgive me?"

"You didn't send me there," says Francisca with lifted head, a look of—what? almost aloofness. "My family did. It wasn't necessary, it was—what Elena calls a *groseria*. But they have never been wise, my family."

"They did it because of me," says Laura. "Because I was afraid of you. It was so stupid of me—" To admit that fear: the hardest thing, even now!

"Laura, they did it because *they* were afraid, don't you know that? Not one of them—not even Andrés—would just talk to me, their own daughter, their own sister!"

"Oh, Francisca." Laura lifts her hand as if to reach for Francisca's. It pauses in air, then falls back into her lap. "And I made it worse. I feel so bad about it."

"It doesn't matter any more." Francisca's eyes glance at the fallen hand, then away. "It was very hard, Laura, but it is over now. And it was my own fault too." Her eyes meet Laura's again. "I was wrong to want to leave Colombia. That *was* a madness. This is my land. The green veins run in my blood. Even this—this murder of my poor Mamá—that is mine to know and understand. It cannot be run away from. It is everywhere. In your country too, you will see."

Laura smiles with relief, with the lifting of guilt. She can't attend to the political things right now. Only one thing matters: "It sounds like you're going to be all right."

"I don't know," says Francisca. "But I am going to be *here*." She leans forward with her old intensity, with a clearer light behind it. "And Laura—there is something else. I am *there* also. I am on the mountains with my *Indios*. Like them I sit in the high, clear air, and I see the wisdom of the ancestors. And I am learning, Laura! I am seeing!"

CHAPTER 41

The Ancestors

"The hospital did not make me better," says Francisca. "My *Indios* made me better. They have given me something. They have changed everything."

The ancestors went so high, you know, that the Spanish could not find them and had to give up killing them. They went so high that they were able to save their beliefs and their ways. Every place on the mountain is sacred to them. The stones are sacred. The air is sacred. In dreams I have climbed up very high, beyond where even the Kogis go, except for their sacred rituals. I passed the last old Priest, sitting on a slab of stone overlooking the valley. I went into the cloud country, where the spirits of the dead return. No animals were there; only a few birds. I thought of Carmen, for a bold hummingbird was there, among the tall ferns. There was no sound, except from a trickle of icy water, from a falling pebble, from my own dreaming blood.

CHAPTER 42

Something New

The family is dealing with its grief, also making plans to dispose of the hotel and find new homes for the sisters and for Tía Marta. Andrés and Laura will return to the United States soon after the funeral. What will happen after that they do not speak of. Laura feels she cannot stay with Andrés much longer. And yet there are the children. And yet she feels a new tenderness for him, after all that has happened. For now everything is in a kind of limbo, a stunned interim. She comforts him slightly, as much as she can. She sits with Tía Marta from time to time. But there is little she can do that doesn't make her feel an intruder in the family's grief.

And so she follows the children's lead, spending time in the kitchen, where Luisa is full of friendliness. She is stout and strong, her cheeks shining in her worn face. It has been Luisa all summer who has told Davy and Susan each night to "duerma con los angeles," to sleep with the angels. As she puts potatoes on to boil in a huge pot, Laura sees how scarred her hands are from years of working in the heat of the huge, coal-burning stove. Yet somehow Luisa manages to work with love. Now, feeling the sorrow of the house, she works all the harder to feed it well.

At this moment, Señor Vargas is also in the kitchen, with his torch and his jewelry equipment. Like Laura, he has been trying not to intrude on the family. Once again, she and the children stand watching as he pours streams of gold accurately into the little forms, making crucifixes and medals of saints. She loves the fascination on Davy's face, the comfort he seems to find in it.

"A terrible thing that happened," Señor Vargas says gently.

"Yes." It is comforting for herself too, watching him along with her Davy, while Susan plays with pot lids nearby and Luisa makes a friendly clatter with her utensils.

"This violence is not the way," Señor Vargas adds, beginning to raise his voice. "To kill an old woman for a few pesos. We cannot meet our problems that way!"

"Davy," she says softly. "I think Luisa is asking for you in kitchen."

"She is?" He is tempted, torn between two attractions.

"I think so," she says. "Maybe she wants Miguel too." And off he runs.

"You don't want the boy to hear these things," observes Señor Vargas.

"No. Not so much anyway. So many hard things in this world! And he is just a little boy who was visiting his grandmother... and then all this! How can he understand what happened to her?"

"You are right, of course."

"How can anyone understand?" she goes on. "When Hilario killed Doña Pilar—he was not thinking about social problems," Laura sinks to the floor, to be eye level with him.

"No. But he was *expressing* them."

"I have wanted to ask you—" Laura hesitates. "When there were bombings of the banks a few weeks ago. Did you—I mean, how did you feel about that?"

"Did I help to do it?" He sets down the torch and laughs, intense little man with a kindly, creased face, crouching there in his cheap, rumpled gray suit. "No, of course I did not! For one thing, I am a coward. And for another, I do not think anything can be accomplished by a few mosquito bites."

"Well what, then?"

He shrugs. "A revolution." His voice slides over the word, with love and irony equally mixed. "But I don't know what a revolution is."

There is a voice from the doorway, Francisca's voice. "I think I know. I have been thinking about this. A revolution is something new. Something *completely new!*"

Señor Vargas smiles at her, as if proud of her. "You are right," he says, "if you mean that the old ways of revolution will not work—just as the old ways of society do not work."

"It means more," says Francisca. "It means we must not think like men and women any more! It means the Kogis on Santa Marta must not talk to the mother goddess in rituals that keep women out, for the goddess will not listen and will not send wisdom. And the Kogis seek wisdom more sincerely than the men in the Capitol and the men in streets with their bombs and their brainwashed women. So what chance do *any* of them have? All of us must think in ways that are new, completely new! We must feel the pure air atop the snowy mountain!"

"I do not understand all that," says Señor Vargas. "I am sure you are right—but all I know is, we must remain alert. Watch. And hope we will recognize the new way when it comes."

"But I am telling you the new way now," says Francisca. "You understand, don't you Laura?"

"I do, Francisca!" Something completely new. The rituals on the mountain, equality starting there, at the highest! I do understand. But what form does that take, what program? What will be the revolution?

Señor Vargas turns off his torch and sits back on his haunches. "But you know," he says, "It is not just our country. We speak of La Violencia and poverty and trouble here. But when you go home to the United States, Laura—you will see things you didn't see before—symptoms of disease, decay. You also—need the completely new, the unknown revolution that Francisca sees so well."

Laura has been thinking something like this herself. Here the lost children, the legless and homeless ones in the street, the barriers against women have been more obvious than at home. But that is because for people like her, things are sheltered or disguised at home. What disturbs here, exists everywhere. No, she will not escape anything by going home. But like Francisca, she no longer wants to escape.

Something else has been saying itself inside her. The beauty of the conch, the mystery of the conch may be on any shore; Francisca's vision on any snowy mountain. Out of these also, perhaps, something completely new. Not easy words, not platitudes, not ancient fears—but something new at least to human minds, because our minds just begin to open to what is always there. That which hums inside the conch spins inside my heart. That which dreams in the mists of the sierra. That which is.

She remembers the beauty of the three nuns alighting on the beach at Cartagena. Such peace she felt, on seeing them. And then—a thought had begun to form in her mind that day, as they took the launch back to the city. She has forgotten it until now. Carmen! Carmen and the nuns.

"Francisca. Señor Vargas." They have been silent for a few moments, listening to the clatter of Luisa's and Susan's pans, smelling the cornmeal scent of baking empanadas.

Both look at her, friendly and alert. "Sí?"

"I was thinking about Carmen. Could we start our revolution with Carmen?"

Señor Vargas bursts into laughter, roars of friendly laughter.

But Francisca already has a hopeful smile on her face, after days of sadness. "Why are you laughing?" she asks him.

Señor Vargas stands up, gasping, and brushes himself off. Little snorts of laughter keep bubbling from him. "I don't know! It seems such a *small* revolution! But no—don't misunderstand. I do not mean to be scornful." He looks composed again, receptive. "But tell me your idea."

"Well," says Laura. "In Cartagena I saw the nuns of St. Vincent de Paul, with their white headdress like birds. I thought that they were very kind and very beautiful. And since there is no place where Carmen can live with real birds as I used to dream for her . . . no aviary . . . ."

"What?" Now Francisca has begun to chuckle. Señor Vargas raises his eyebrows in a carefully sober, smiling way.

"You'll think this is . . ."

"Laura, go on!" says Francisca. She moves into the room, closer, so that the three of them are standing like conspirators on a street corner.

"All right." Laura shifts her feet a little, making room, feeling a circle take form. "I thought since Carmen loves birds, maybe she would like to live with the nuns who wear birds on their heads!" Even Laura laughs a bit now. A whimsy, a Thumbelina ending. A comic dream. No, that can't be all. "For a time, I mean. Until maybe—maybe you could bring her to me in the States, Francisca, if she wants to come?"

"It is a good idea," says Señor Vargas, wiping his eyes. "The Church is of the past, of the never-new. But the sweet Vincentían nuns, they are all right. Perhaps Carmen will be good for them too! She'll make things new, she'll be our spy," he says grandly, grinning.

"No," says Francisca.

Laura is surprised, hurt. "No, Francisca?"

"It is a good idea, Laura," she says. "But don't you see? The nuns may be like birds, but they are captive birds. I have been the captive bird too, I know about that. It is not good enough for Carmen."

"But Francisca, we can't leave her where she is."

"No," says Francisca. "Don't you see? You have just made *me* see. Carmen can stay with me!"

"But Francisca, how—" Señor Vargas makes a little coughing noise, a polite hesitation.

"With Tía Marta and me," she says. "Oh, don't worry—" she meets the inquiry in his eye. "I will never hit her like I once hit the maids. When I am afraid or sad—I will never again say so by hitting someone. And Carmen—she will not be anybody's servant, not ever." Francisca's voice, so sure and confident, drops into shyness, surprise at what she is finding to say: "She will be like my child, my found child."

Laura allows the power of her feeling to sit in silence. She looks at Francisca's gleaming eyes, her wild and confident grin. She listens with a heart full of sudden and powerful hope, with a big, drawn-in breath, the air singing through her.

"You will help me, Laura? You and my brother will help us? Carmen must go to school. She must not make lace with Tía Marta and me. She must have choices."

This is when Laura reaches across the new circle, reaches for both Francisca's hands and feels the energy pulsing between them, between her hands and Francisca's. "You too, Francisca," she says. "Everyone must have choices, even if we spin them out of nowhere." Out of dreams or mysteries, or vague good impulses that turn into strong, sure acts like this.

"That is easy for now," says Francisca. "While she needs me—I choose Carmen."

CHAPTER 43

The Hummingbird

The hummingbird was the master of water. It was a magical bird, and could find water in the nectar of the flowers or in small rock pools high in the mountains where no flowers grew. Because it was so small, no one thought to ask it how it found water. But one dry season when thirst was very powerful, they watched it, iridescent violet and green, much too beautiful for anything in that season of thirsting.

"What is your secret, hummingbird?" they asked. But it only replied, "My secret is that I am already spinning toward the form souls take when they die. I find water because I have gone beyond all seasons of dryness." They tried to capture it and make it lead them to water, but it was so small that it flew through their nets. And if they came to snatch it by hand where it fed at the nectar of a flower, suspended on its spinning, invisible wings, it would fly up into a wonderful backwards somersault in air, and disappear.

CHAPTER 44

Out of the Conch Shell

In her room late that night, Andrés not yet there, Laura watches Susan sleeping, dreaming. Little puckers of worry and sadness move across her rosy, cherubic face. And at the other end of the bed David, sleeping with his arms flung behind his head, as if he had just fallen from the sky. Qué duerma con los angeles! Beloved little ones, born so mysteriously into this strange conjunction of cultures and lives! What will you learn, what will you bring to the future?

Laura opens the big wardrobe by her bed and takes from the bottom back corner, behind her dress-up shoes, the wrinkled pages of *El Tiempo*, the old headlines, the ads for lost children, all pressed and crumpled around one solid, spiky weight. The soft crinkling causes Susan to moan slightly, to stir, then sigh.

Laura draws out the conch shell, like a small temple of wisdom, brought back from Cartagena. Leaving the pile of papers in the bottom of the wardrobe, she climbs back onto the bed with her treasure. She holds it to her ear. It is almost as large as her head, as if it is another head listening at her ear, the way she listens to it. Whose secrets will be whispered?

She sets it down, her hand trembling, almost a buzzing in her fingers. No longer afraid, Laura picks up her notebook, her pen. She holds the pen loosely upright, and immediately it begins to glide across the page in large, round, primitive handwriting, plucked out of the air. Slowly at first, then faster and faster

I am only your wisdom in a different voice, the fear was your fear in a different voice too.

Love is the last word I write to you. Let it not become your tie to heaven or your tie to earth alone. Let it be god's ribbon linking the souls in elegant gestures. Hear it, let it work in you, let it keep you strong. And fear no more, for the death of fear is the gift of

Love

Love is scrawled very large, it takes up half a page. Sky-writing. It disperses in the blue, it becomes cloud ribbons, linking the souls in elegant gestures. The pen falls from Laura's hand. Warmly, drowsily, as if she has been lovingly held for a long time, she slides the notebook under her bed, and places the conch shell over it in benediction, bene-listening. She sleeps with the angels.

CHAPTER 45

Rebirth

"I know my Mamá will have a funeral in the Church," says Francisca. "But in my heart, she will also have a funeral on the Sierra Nevada de Santa Marta. The religions melt together, when you are alone for a long time in a dark place. And on the mountain I have seen more than I ever saw before."

The wind is cold. A mist hangs over the mountain. Only a few mourners are present—only the family. Tía Marta is there in her wheelchair. Carmen stands next to her, her hand touching the silvery wheel. The rest of us stand beside and around them. Papá stands in the mist, composed and respectful. Further away our frail uncle stands. Mamá's first husband.

The priest of the Kogi in his white robe, with his strong, handsome face and long hair, stands before us. He speaks these words at the beginning of the ceremony: "This is the village of Death; this is the ceremonial house of Death; this is the uterus. I am now going to open the house." Then with his shovel he moves some soil from East to West, from West to East; from North to South, from South to North. "The house is open."

Men begin to dig the circular grave. Our mother lies in the position of an unborn child, wrapped in white cotton cloth. He sews the cloth around her, leaving only the hair of her head outside the cloth. We tie a fiber rope to her hair. Then our mother is lifted into a carrying net.

Tía Marta begins to chant a wailing song, a dirge. The rest of us join her. There is sorrow in the chant, but no words. There is longing and hope, but no words. Now we bring forth small bundles of leaves, with shells in them, small spiral shells and others. We speak to the shells, calling them "food for the dead," and place them in the carrying net with our mother.

The priest of the Kogi steps solemnly into the grave, holding small bundles made of leaves. Slowly he unties them and takes out of them crushed stones, seeds, fibers of cotton. These he leaves in the center of the grave, and then steps out of it again. Now he goes to the body of our mother. He prepares himself to lift it, and we watch with great tension. It is very heavy. He can barely lift it, and he puts it on the earth again. There is silence among us. He begins to lift it again, but on his face is a look of doubt. On the third try, the body of Mamá has become a little less heavy, and the priest smiles, to let us know. Again and again he lifts it, and each time it becomes lighter. We begin to feel relieved, for all will be well. When he lifts it the ninth time, it is very light, like a newborn baby or a fragile shell from the sea. He is smiling, and we all look at each other with relief. Tía Marta wipes her eyes with her handkerchief.

The priest asks Andrés to place our Mamá's body in the grave. Then we all bring armfuls of green fern, which we spread lovingly over her, remembering how she loved trees and growing things. Now the men begin to fill the grave with earth, but always taking care to see that the rope tied to Mamá's hair will not be buried. When the grave is covered and only the rope emerges from the earth, a stick is placed upright in the ground nearby, and the rope is pulled tight and twisted around the stick. All of these things have happened in silence.

Now the priest closes the uterus, the house of Death, by moving some earth again, this time from South to North, from North to South; from West to East, and from East to West. He dismisses us all, showing us how to walk away from the funeral rite in a winding, spiraling motion. In this way we untie the thread of death. We become invisible to death and to evil influences. We twirl on our own cosmic center, as we move away. I push Tía Marta's wheelchair before me in the same spiral motion. She smiles, and we twirl around and around, Carmen clinging to my skirt, running beside.

On the ninth day, we return. During this time our mother's soul has been wandering on dangerous paths, but she is nourished by the offerings we left with her. Now that we return on the ninth day, we find the priest of the Kogi waiting for us. He pulls on the rope that extends from the grave, and it breaks. He smiles at us. All of us smile, for our mother has been safely reborn in another world.

CHAPTER 46

Carmen

It is the night before the funeral. Francisca appears in the dining room with Carmen.

"Andrés," she says, "Carmen wants to eat with David and Susan. Help me to put these tables together?"

Andrés gets up eagerly from the table where he sits with Laura and the children. He has wanted all summer to do this. He pulls Francisca and Elena's table over. Yes, it is about an inch higher. And too late for him to bother leveling it. No matter.

Laura lifts Elena's little tray of condiments, sets it down again, where the two tables meet, on Elena's side. She and Francisca move the chairs around. It is exhilarating to do this little thing, put these two small pieces together!

Susan is chortling with delight. "Eat 'side Carmen!" she demands.

Carmen is very shy. How has she come here? What is happening, that she should be among them in this new way? She is warm in the sweater Laura gave her, and underneath it a warm green dress that Francisca and Laura got her before they came home. Even her legs are warm in new tights they bought for her. In the room upstairs is a little unfinished mourning dress that Francisca is making out of an old skirt. And Francisca has brought to the table her lace maker's bag, which contains inside it something wonderful: a lace collar that is being made very quickly, just for Carmen to wear tomorrow.

Andrés is looking at Laura. "Shall we move Concha's table too?"

"Let's try it," she says.

They are just pulling it out from the wall when Concha walks in with her baby on her hip, little Miguel walking behind her. "What is this?"

"We want to include you," says Andrés.

"Mamá is not even in the grave," she says, "and you dishonor her like this!"

"No dishonor," says Andrés. "I wanted to suggest it to her all summer. Some day I would have. And now, it's because the children want to sit together."

"That one!" Concha looks at Carmen, sitting on a cushion now, next to Susan. "Do you think I would let my child sit next to a servant?"

"Conchita," says Andrés. "Be kind. You know Francisca wants to make Carmen her own child, to teach her, to give her a chance. She is going to be part of our family now."

"She is not only a servant, she is a freak." Concha has the decency to almost whisper this, as if she has some slight perception that Carmen may have feelings. "I cannot permit it."

"You cannot stop it," says Francisca in full, firm voice. "Please remember that, Concha. And honor Mamá with your kindness—Mamá who was rough and stern, but she would hire people with no working papers, just to give them a chance!"

"And look what it got her," says Concha. "What a stupid thing for you to say! A bleeding throat is what it got her!"

Andrés slides into his chair rapidly. The mention of blood at any time makes him faint. That Concha can speak of his mother's—he cannot even think it. He puts his hands on the table to keep himself upright.

"Andrés, are you all right?" whispers Laura.

"Sí. In a moment," he says.

CHAPTER 47

Procession

On the afternoon of the funeral it is raining lightly. Each of the cars for the procession has a wreath of rain-freshened flowers on top, by custom ornate and extravagant, even though there are only a few mourners: Pilar's children and a few old friends, a few cousins.

Before they climb into the car, Laura, holding Susan in one arm, touches the wreath with her free hand. Rosy pink, gold, lilac, white. Like spring. Drops of rain are trembling on the flowers. Susan reaches up a questing little hand, and Laura helps her to touch the wreath also.

"Me too," says David, and she sets Susan down for a moment, picks up her big five-year-old, and holds him up to the car roof, where he touches the flowers tenderly. "They're pretty," he says, as she gently lowers him to the ground.

"You're getting bigger, Davy!" she tells him, shaking her arms out and grinning at him.

"Now me!" says Susan, and up she goes again, patting the flowers.

"I will see you at the Church," says Andrés, as he helps them into the car with Francisca and Carmen. "Don't worry about what Concha said," he says to Francisca. "You know how she is." His body, his gestures, seem to have grown lighter with sadness, but his face heavier, his long cheeks furrowed like an old man's.

"She should have more kindness," says Francisca.

"Well—" Andrés offers a smile. "Maybe it is good for you to have one person left to fight with."

Francisca gives a short laugh. "Maybe so! Anyway, Andrés, thank you for what you said to her. And be kind to yourself today."

Laura, settling the children, smiles at Andrés as he shuts the door. She is feeling not just sad for him, but a new pride for him too, because he defended Carmen and Francisca. He nods with his sad face, then walks to the car ahead of them, where they will ride with Concha and Elena.

Now Carmen, squeezed between Laura and Francisca, holds Susan's hand and looks up at Laura with a sharp little smile beaming above her new lace collar. How can she be sad when there is so much for her to celebrate?

As they wait for the procession to begin, Laura looks out the rain-beaded window. On the opposite sidewalk maybe thirty girls, dressed in frothy white, are walking in double file to their first communion. Each girl carries a candle, struggling to protect it from the rain without losing her step in a stately march that has no music. Their eyes have a solemn, holy look, perhaps from the effort of keeping their candles alight in the rain. Hugging Susan in her lap, one arm around Davy who is squeezed cosily between her and Francisca, Laura brushes her wet cheeks against her daughter's warm, curly hair.

"Do not cry, Laura," says Francisca. "Carmen and I will take care of each other. We will be all right. And you know—I have already mourned Mamá in my own way."

Laura looks at Francisca's rough, kind face and smiles. "Yes," she says vaguely, thinking of Francisca and Carmen, but still thinking, too, of those little girls. Like white silken fluff, nestled in milkweed pods so neatly, soon to drift out anywhere, anyhow—

"And even if you are not always my brother's wife—"

Shock—that Francisca has guessed such a thought. But hesitantly, softly, Laura answers. "I don't know . . . maybe . . .

maybe not." Whatever happens, she thinks, we can respect each other now, and even more, perhaps, if we ever part.

"I know, Laura. I just mean that it's all right. That's why I want to tell you: whatever happens, you will still be my sister."

"Oh yes—Always." But Laura cannot tell Francisca how much it means to hear that. She laughs and reaching past David, she cups her hand gently at the crown of Carmen's shining head, sliding it over that sweet corner-curve of heat and spirit at the back of a growing child's head. "And Carmen's aunt!"

David twists and grins. "Carmen!" he says, and she smiles back at him.

"Yes. And you little ones will be cousins." Francisca's eyes are gentle. Her warrior mouth like her brother's, her bold adventurer's mouth that is only Francisca's, is serene now, her lips poised gently, almost lightly, between sadness and joy.

"Mira, Davy! Susan! Look!" Now Carmen has caught sight of the line of girls in their communion dresses. She joggles David's knee to point them out to him.

"Another parade?!" he looks out in astonishment.

"Ohhhh!" Susan laughs and Carmen giggles with her.

Francisca's gaze follows the children's laughing attention, finds the girls in their communion dresses. "Do you see them, Laura?"

"Sí. I have been looking at them," she says. Their sweet, dark eyes and the lacy whiteness of their dresses against the rain-darkened day. Laura feels the slow spinning of life within them all. It rises, whirling from within, brimming over.

She turns again to Francisca. "We'll find ways to help each other, I know. I'll send you something every month for Carmen, as soon as I have a job." She hears herself say that. She pauses a moment, takes its meaning in. Whatever happens, work of her own, a job of her own. "And Andrés, too," she says softly. "I'll remind him. And you'll write to me about Carmen's studies, we'll—" Laura meets her sister's eye. A funny look there makes her laugh and shake her tears away over Susan's lively curls, over her little boy's head so full of thoughts. Because of course, Francisca has no more use for weeping.

Giant heart, giant wings.

AFTERWORD

Condor and Hummingbird was first published in 1986, by Alice Walker's Wild Trees Press, under my former name, Charlotte Méndez. (A United Kingdom edition was published in 1987 by The Women's Press.) It was inspired by my experiences in Colombia in 1963, and my interest in the mythology of the Kogi of Santa Marta. So far as I know, it remains one of the few works of fiction to engage with the culture of the Kogi, who I first learned about while living in Colombia. The references to the Kogi of Santa Marta in this novel are based on Gerardo Reichel-Dolmatoff's article on funerary customs of the Kogi in *Native South Americans*, edited by Patricia Lyon (Boston: Little Brown, 1974), and on the description of the Kogi in *The Cocaine Eaters*, by Brian Moser and Donald Tayler (New York: Taplinger, 1967). After my novel was published, I came across *The Heart of the World*, the wonderful BBC film by Alan Ereira, which depicts the warning the Kogi, as "elder brother" give to their "younger brother" (ourselves), about the way we are destroying the environment. I recommend this remarkable work, and Ereira's more recent film *Aluna,* to any readers who would like to learn more about the Kogi.

The "myths" in the novel, although of my own creation, and meant to represent some of the characters in the story, are inspired by actual South American Indian myths and symbols reported in *From Honey to Ashes*, by Claude Levi-Strauss (New York: Harper & Row, 1973).

Reissuing *Condor and Hummingbird* thirty years after its initial publication has been an interesting experience for me. The "present moment" that I remember writing about in a little diary on the train between Bogotá and Cartagena in 1963, and tried to recapture in a novel that I wrote during the 1970's and early '80s, has now become a lost moment in history. And yet in some ways the world hasn't changed; political violence, social injustice, and the plight of "lost children" are as much with us now as they were thirty years ago

Most personally, for me this work of fiction about an American wife and mother's visit to her husband's homeland always had one sorrowful flaw: in distancing it from my own experience, I gave Laura only one child, a little girl. Years later, I remember apologizing to my late son David Méndez because there was no little boy in the story, though in real life he had been very much present. He just laughed at that idea, and yet I always felt that Susan in the story was missing her big brother. And so this edition has one major revision: the presence of a five-year-old boy named David, alongside his little sister. Really, he was there all along.

Charlotte Zoë Walker

CHARLOTTE ZOË WALKER is a former NEA Fellow in Creative Writing, and O. Henry Award winner. In addition to *Condor and Hummingbird*, she has published numerous essays and short stories, including "The Very Pineapple" (*Prize Stories 1991: The O. Henry Awards*), and "Goat's Milk" (listed among "100 Distinguished Stories" in *Best American Short Stories, 1993*). She is the editor of two books on naturalist John Burroughs published by Syracuse University Press: *Sharp Eyes* and *The Art of Seeing Things*. She lives with her husband, Dutch ironsmith Roland Greefkes, on a hillside in upstate New York that is visited by many hummingbirds, but no condors.

29330083R00102

Made in the USA
Middletown, DE
16 February 2016